This is a work of fiction. Names, characters, businesses, places, events and incidents are either the product of the writers imagination or used in a fictitious manner. Any resemblance to actual persons, living, or dead, or actual events are pure coincidental.

PAPERBACK VERSION
ISBN-13: 978-0578150208
ISBN-10: **0578150204**
BIASC: FICTION/URBAN

Published by EducatedThugPublications LLC
Cover Art: AMB BRANDING AND DESIGN

TO ORDER ADDITIONAL COPIES OR OTHER WORKS CONTACT:
Facebook: Street Royalty. Instagram: @educatedthugpub
www.EducatedThug-Publications.com

Prologue

Back when I was just a tiny little girl, I used to dream of having a storybook wedding: in a big church, jam-packed with all my closest friends and family, surrounded by loads of love and dozens of lavender roses and lilies. Yes, I could see clearly the white fluffy strapless gown that fell beautifully to the ground, the thick honey-blonde tresses that flowed from the top of my innocent head down to the soft yellow skin of my shoulders, and the satisfied glint in my emerald green eyes, as I watched my handsome hubby slide the monstrous wedding ring down my finger. Yes, I could see it all. Had it mapped out too! Including, but not limited to, which particular pastor would preside over the service, and which of my hubby's friends would serve as best man. Some say I was a little obsessed with marriage and all its associated trimmings, but, in the end, what is a little girl's life without dreams and wishes?

It was nearly twelve years later—now twenty years old—when I watched all my dreams manifest: the flowers, the beautiful dress, the tresses that fell down onto my bare yellow shoulders, even the huge monstrous wedding ring. Everything was perfect. Everything was just as I had planned. Everything except for my husband.

I never anticipated marrying a gangster. I never asked—or even wanted—to be involved his mannish lifestyle. All I wanted was love, respect, and affection; for him to be my best friend and companion; my knight in shining armor; my everything and more. But, I guess we don't always get what we want or desire from life. We do live and we learn though. We live, we learn, we grow.

"The streets are war… 'Till death do you part." It took me years to understand the truth behind this ice-cold motto. I learned the hard way, too. I learned through my own flesh, blood, and tears. I learned that no matter directly or indirectly, once the streets get ahold of you, its virtually impossible to free yourself. I learned that the streets are unsympathetic, that they gnaw and tear at you, ripping you away from all things humane. Then—Then, when you're no good to anyone or anything—when you're literally clinging onto your life, within your last dying breaths, the streets slit your throat and watch your blood seep out onto the unforgiving concrete.

As you can see, I think nothing good of the streets. And why should I? The streets represent insanity; They're the devil's playground. It's a lose-lose situation. Every man, woman, and child associated with the streets receives the same thing: death, despair, destruction. The streets are the deep abyss from where every ounce of pain, suffering, and agony comes from, and if not for my husband, I would've never come to know The Big Bad Streets. I would've never come to know the price and particular measurements of drugs such as cocaine and heroin, never known the sordid stench associated with death, nor would I be able to genuinely express what it felt to be kidnapped and beat within an inch of my life.

Many people say I'm lucky to be alive. I say I'm blessed. I know only a small percentage of people are fortunate to say that they've escaped the murderous and vengeful grasp of the streets, and to that I say my life and situation is a work of God; a miracle. And how do I repay Him for this miracle? I say the best way is to pay it forward and share my testimony. Each one teach one.

So, that said, to all of you women out there whom are particularly fond of your gangsters and dopeboys, please— please you all—take the time out of your lives to actually assess who and what you're dealing with. The streets are relentless and unbiased. They take, and they take, giving little back in return.

We only have one life. Live it and live it gracefully. After all, *Everybody Dies, But Not Everybody Lives...*

<u>Chapter One</u>

I was fresh out of high school when my older cousin and legal guardian, Remy, offered me a job bartending at his nightclub, Aphrodisiac. Initially I was quite hesitant. As of that time I'd only been out clubbing twice in my entire eighteen years on earth, and both nights were utterly unforgettable. With all the shouting, fighting, and shooting, it's a wonder anyone had a good time. By twelve midnight I was totally scared out of my wits, vowing to never visit another club as long as I lived. Not even my cousins place. While I sat at the kitchen table texting an old friend, Remy popped the question.

"Why don't you come on down to the club and give me a hand with things, Jordyn. You know I could use the help."

"Hun-unh. I'm not working at a nightclub. Thanks, but no thanks. I'll pass."

"Why not?" he asked while pouring himself a tall glass of orange juice. "You know you could use the money. How else you gonna keep up wit' the latest trends in fashion and technology? Don't trip, it'll be cool."

"Once again, I'll pass."

"C'mon Jordyn, why you makin' this so difficult? I really need you."

I texted the last few characters in my message and shoved the phone into my Dayton Flyers hoodie pocket. I always dressed down on Sundays; sweatpants, flip-flops, and hoodies. "No, Remy. I told you before that clubs scare the crap out me."

5

"And I told you that you'd be okay."

"But I'd still be uncomfortable. And besides," I said, eager to take some of the seriousness out of the early morning convo, "why are you so amp'd up about hiring me anyway? Isn't the country still under a recession?" I asked playfully.

Remy flashed me a plastic smile. "Funny, Jordyn. Real fuckin' funny."

"Oh. Someone is very agitated this morning. Profanity? And at this hour? Whoa, I better warn the troops."

Remy's facial expression remained unmoved. "I'm serious, Jordyn. I really need you."

I took to the cookie jar and fetched out one of my cousin Tish's amazing homemade peanut butter cookies. "Why? Why do you need little ol' me so bad, Remy? Huh? There must be something up your sleeve if you're so desperate."

"I'm not des—I'm not desperate. I just need you. Shit, and why are you putting me through all of this anyway? Why can't you just say yes and let that be that?

"Because, I know you're leaving something out. That's why. Now be truthful, why do you need me there so bad?"

No matter how hard he tried, Remy just couldn't lie to me. He couldn't. He once told me it had something to do with my big green eyes, the innocence in them.

"It's just... I uh... Well, I uh," he stuttered.

"The truth, Remy. I want the truth," I reminded.

"Shit, Jordyn. You got me feelin' like I'm on trial for murder or some shit. Why you doin' me like this? All I do for you? All I'm askin' for is a lil' help."

"Quit stallin'," I said with my finger pointed at him. "The truth, please."

Remy slammed back the remainder of the OJ and grunted. He placed the glass inside of the dishwasher.

I cleared my throat, again. "Couldn't hear you."

Another grunted mumble.

"Jesus. You get on my nerves sometimes, Jordyn... Beauty. There. You happy? I said it. Beauty."

"Beauty? Beauty?" I repeated, half lost as to what he was implying. "Ooh, you tryna pimp out your own flesh 'n' blood!" I yelled. "You wait until I tell Tish," I threatened. "You wait!"

Remy fanned me off the way you'd fan a bold-faced liar. "Girl ain't nobody trying to pimp you out. And my wife would never believe you."

I rolled my eyes and smacked my lips dramatically. "Boy bye. Tish'll believe anything I tell 'er, and you know it."

Remy paused before adding very defiantly, "Yeah, you're right. But on the serious side, I need you, Jay-Jay."

"I thought you already had two good lookin' girls working for you down there. What, they can't mix or something?"

"Oh, no. They're damn good bartenders."

"What's the problem then? They stealin'? 'Cause if they stealin' I'll come down there and straighten 'em out." I threw a flurry of punches at the air and quickly swooped an errand strand of hair from my face. Although I'd never been in a real physical altercation before, I'd say that I had good enough posture and agility to fight my cousin's battle for him.

"No, they're not stealing, Jordyn." By now Remy was pacing the black and white tiled kitchen floor.

"What is it then?" I spat with an obvious flare of irritation prevalent in my tone.

"They're ugly!"

"Ugly?"

"Yeah, ugly" he repeated.

01I burst out in laughter. "You mean to tell me you don't want them around anymore because they're ugly? But didn't you hire them?

"No, not just ugly, but hideous. And no, I didn't hire them. Your cousin did."

"Who, Tish? Oh, now I understand." I laughed. "It all makes senses now. Well, I guess you picked your own poison... Live with the results of your actions, Mr. Man."

"Oh, so now you're quoting me, huh?"

"Yup," I said and took a nibble of my cookie, looking down at it. "A man of many great words... I should start calling you Dr. Martin Luther King The Fourth."

"I guess you're a comedian too now, huh? Well, let's see who's doin' all the laughin' when yo' high-yellow-ass out on the curb; see who laughin' then."

I couldn't help laughin' in his face. By now I was bent over clutching my stomach, tears streamin' from my eyes.

"Oh, so you gone just laugh in my face. You know what? Get the hell out of my house. Get Out!" Remy said with his finger trained at the front door. "Go 'head, get! Get!" he shooed.

8

I nearly choked on a laughter bubble. "You can't—you can't kick me out," I said between hiccups of laughter. "I live here, fool."

"Not anymore. You know the drill: If you ain't for us, you against us. And you damn sure ain't for us right now. Get out. Now!"

I laughed so hard that a tinkle of pee dribbled out in my panties. If I didn't hurry and stop him I'd piss my pants completely.

To be honest, I knew from the very moment Remy asked me to help him out that I would. I mean, even though I didn't really wanna, I could never deny Remy anything; he nor his wife Tish. They became my surrogate parents when my parents were killed. Everything I ever wanted in life they gave me. They provided a good upbringing for me. I went to the best private school in our region, adorned all the latest trends in fashions and technology, and pretty much had free reign to come and go as I pleased—that is, of course, after I reached a responsible age and level of maturity.

Overall, Remy and Tish were fantastic in raising me. Therefore, I'd never be able to deny them. I just wanted to see Remy sweat.

"Okay, I'll do it," I said. Remy's mouth dropped as if he couldn't believed I changed my mind.

"Really?" he asked with his arms spread out.

I smiled, "Yeah, I just wanted to see you sweat. You know I could never deny you or Tish anything."

Remy jumped in the air and yelled. "Ahhh! That's what I'm talkin' 'bout Jay-Jay." He reached out to hug me but I stopped him.

"No. Wait. You have to promise me two things first."

"Anything. Anything, just name it!" I knew from Remy's extreme level of excitement that he really needed me. And he was prepared to pay anything. Even a king's ransom. But I'd never exploit family. Family is all we have in life. When the money and fame fade all we have is family.

"Two things … First" I held with my finger raised, clearly exhibiting my dominance in the situation, "You have'ta keep the other two women on."

Remy's face contorted. "What! Aw hell naw. Those ugly bitches the same ones bringing down my stock. Hell no. Hu-unh."

"You have to, Remy. I won't do it unless you do it."

"Why? You don't even know those bitches. Why you carin' so much about dem hoes?"

I slapped his arm for his obvious contempt and disrespect for the two black women he employed.

"I know I don't know them, but it'll kill me knowing somebody lost their job because of me. I can't have that on my conscience Remy, I just can't."

Remy dropped his head dismally. "And the other?" he asked.

I walked up and straightened the collar on Remy's white and blue cotton button-up shirt. "The other is, I need you to promise me you'll protect me from any danger Remy."

Remy looked down at me through squinted eyes. "Clubs scare the crap out of me. They really do."

Remy hugged and kissed me on the top of my head.

"Jordyn, you know I'd never let anything happen to you. Not only are you my little cousin, but you're like my daughter. I've watched you blossom from a itty-bitty little girl with big green eyes and bucked teeth into an intelligent, beautiful young woman with a long life ahead of her." Remy hugged me tighter and kissed me on top of the head again. "Big cuz got yo' back."

Remy stepped back and gave me a once over, eyeing my loose-fitting jogging pants and hoodie. "Now c'mon," he said with a nudge of my shoulder, "let's get you to Macy's so we can get you a mini-skirt and shoulderless top to set off that sex appeal. He winked his eye and laughed. "Everbody know that Remy pimpin'! C'mon now girl, you my bottom chick. Time is money, you play wit' my money and I'ma play wit yo' life!"

<u>Chapter Two</u>

3 Months Later

The club scene turned out to be not so bad after all. Probably because Remy's place was totally different from the other two places I visited in the past. Club Aphrodisiac, with its warm, rich colors and tapestries, and its soft leather sofas and matching booths, paled in comparison.

Club Aphrodisiac was beautiful. Michelle and Unique—my cousin's two alleged hideous bartenders— were beautiful people, too. They were very useful in memorizing the different bottles of liquor and mixing. Honestly, I don't know what I would've done without them. They were genuine. I really liked them.

One of the best things about Aphrodisiacs was the crowd it catered to. With a required age limit of 35 and older, and a strict dress code of no baseball caps or gym shoes, it eliminated a lot of riffraff. I mean, there were a few "obvious gangsters" who slipped by, but overall, we catered to a very suave and laid back crowd. And thank God! Lord knows I couldn't have dealt with a bunch of gun-toting, doo-rag wearing thugs. At that point I'd never had an urge or enticement to be in their company, and I definitely wanted to keep it that way. Some women want nothing to do with a man if he's not a thug or gangster. I was the exact opposite. Sagging pants, gold teeth, excessive jewelry, crazy hair-styles or vehicles—all of these were an instant deterrent to me. And although I hadn't quite figured out exactly what qualities I wanted in a man, I was sure the aforementioned weren't in the category. I wanted a *real* man.

It didn't take me very long to get the hang of things around the club. Didn't take long to get a little clientele either. According to Remy, I managed to boost sales "exceptionally" in the ninety days I was there. I believe he was over-exaggerating a bit, but who was I to call him on it?

"They love you!" Remy exclaimed as I handed one of my customers a drink. "I told you they were gon' love you! We back on top, baby!" he said in my ear.

I smiled, scooped up my tip, and waited until my customer walked off before I turned to him. "Don't you think you're over-exaggerating a little bit Remy?"

"Over-exaggerating? Don't you see? Look at the bar. Look at the booths. All these people are here 'cause of you. They all came out to see the new bartender at Aphrodisiac. They're your fans, Jordyn." Remy flashed a big grin then leaned in closer. "And, like I said before, beauty sales!"

*   *   *

I made good money working at Aphrodisiacs. So much that, within six months I was able to buy a new car (well, new to me) and move out on my own. Of course Tish was devastated that I was moving out, but what did she expect? For me to stay there until I was thirty?

Tish must have known the day was fast approaching. My nineteenth birthday was near and she knew I had plans on being out by my birthday. I guess, much like my decision of taking 2-3 years off before enrolling in college, although Tish had to respect it, she didn't like it. But, like it says in the Good Book, everything has its own season, and Mama Tish was just gonna have to deal with it. Bottom line.

I did good for my very first apartment; two bedrooms, wall-to-wall carpeting, all stainless steel appliances, a balcony overlooking a lot of bright-green pastures, an Olympic sized swimming pool, two full-sized gyms, and a tennis court. I instantly fell in love with my new place. God was definitely being good to me.

After the movers left I made myself a cup of Chocolate Mandingo Chai Tea and was somewhere deep in La-La land when my cell phone rang.

I knew immediately from the ring tone who the caller was, and, funny as it may sound, exactly what they wanted. It was Tish, and she was undoubtedly calling to see how things were going in my new environment. How motherly of she.

I picked up the phone and pressed talk. "Hey, Tish."

"Hey, baby. The movers came yet?" She was so sweet and so motherly that I couldn't help but think what my biological mother would've been like.

"Yes, Mama Tish," I said smiling "They done came and left already."

She smacked her lips. "And?"

I smiled harder. "And what?"

"And, is everything okay?" she asked pressingly.

"Well, not really," I led on.

"What's wrong? What'd they do? I told you you should've went with the other company."

"Jeeze, calm down."

"Well, if they broke or stole something we need to report them right now. Ain't no need in letting time pass. It makes the claim look questionable. We need to get on it now—"

"Tish?"

"—getting around to those people. I know their kind. They think just because I'm middle class that I ain't gone make no fuss. Well, child, first of all I'm a Sista and—"

"Tish?" I huffed into the phone. That got her attention.

"Yes, baby, what is it?" she asked in a concerned tone of voice.

"Everything's okay," I confirmed. "You don't have'ta turn anybody in. Everything's cool."

"Well, why did you just say everything wasn't okay? I thought something was wrong."

"I just…well," I said and looked back into my living room. "I just think I probably should've had 'em move the chaise to the other side of the room." I tilted my head to the side and the vision materialized. I smacked my lips. "Dang. I'm definitely gonna have'ta move it to the other side."

Sniffles emanated from the opposite end of the phone.

"Tish? You okay?"

"Yeah, I'm okay," she managed to utter in between sniffles.

"No you're not. Why are you crying? What's wrong?"

She sniffled again.

"What's wrong, Tish? Come on now, spit it out."

A brief moment passed before Tish came clean. "My baby done grown up on me," she said with a slight laugh. Tish was undoubtedly dabbing her eyes while she spoke. "I thought this day would never come. My Jay-Jay done finally grew up on me. Awww..."

"Don't worry, Mama Tish. I'll be over every other day to torment you and Remy. Trust me. You're not gettin' rid of me that easy."

"You say that now. But what's gonna happen when you finally get you some you-know-what? Then what?"

I smacked my lips. "Girl, bye. I told you that's the last thing on my mind. Some man laying on top of me."

"Umh. And who ever said it'd be that position? See, I told you you were ready. That little box between your legs drivin' you crazy. You can tell me. I won't judge you. I lost my virginity at seventeen, so I sho' can't say nothing. But be honest with me, you're ready aren't you?"

"No," I said defensively, "I'm not. That's the last thing on my mind, I told you that."

"Um-hm, told me you'd wait 'till you were nineteen before you moved out too. So is that the truth too?"

I laughed. "Tish, my birthday is in ninety days."

"I know, heifer. I done spent it with you the last fourteen years. What you tryna be funny?"

I chuckled. That was special. Tish was in her feelings about me moving. Told you she'd be.

"No, I'm not trying to be funny. And I thank you for all that you and Cousin Remy done for me," I said seriously. "I wouldn't be the woman I am without you two."

"But? Go on and say it."

"But, it was time. I needed to get out and spread my wings"

"And your legs," she said through a playful cough.

"Whatever. I heard that," I shot back. " But, seriously, I'll forever be indebted to you two. And, you have my word that, when—if!—I decide to ever have sex, that I'll be responsible and protect myself."

"You better. What are the two things I always tell you to avoid doing, contracting an STD and what?"

"And bringing a child into an unstable environment," I repeated in a voice and tone that mimicked an irritated adolescent child.

"That's right," Tish commented in satisfaction. "That's absolutely right… Well, I'm not gonna hold you up. Make sure you call me when you get all set up over there. Maybe I can come through and drop off my housewarming gift. Maybe we can go have dinner or something."

"Sounds good to me."

"M-kay. Love you baby."

"Love you too. Call you later."

After hanging up with Tish, I moved the chaise, took a nice long hot shower, and settled in watching re-runs of The Housewives of Atlanta until it was time for me to go to work. And I knew I probably should've gotten a little shut eye, but, what more could I say: Ms. Thang was finally moving up in the world.

Amen!

<u>Chapter Three</u>

Tuesday nights in Club Aphrodisiac were designated ladies nights, which quite typically brought in a much larger crowd. By ten p.m. the crowd was fair. By twelve midnight we were at our capacity; both dance floors were overflowing with patrons, as well as the tables, booths, sofas, and bar area of the club. Tuesday nights were the most chaotic night of the week for me. Come Monday, I was already regretting what the next twenty-four hours would bring. Sounded fun, huh?

"Girl, it seems like they ain't gone stop coming!" I said to Unique, a fair-skinned heavy set woman of thirty-five years. She was standing next to me behind the bar watching me make drink after drink for my customers. "I must've made at least four-hundred drinks."

Unique kinda scoffed. "Hmp. Lord knows I need that kind play right now. With all these doctor's bills, and home health care, I'm falling seriously behind. Shit, I wish they took to me like that."

I reached into my apron pocket and grabbed a handful of crumpled bills. "Here. This'll help out."

Unique looked down at the wad of money and pressed my hand away. "No. I can't do that Jordyn. You worked too damn hard for your money. I'll manage."

Unique had a five year old handicapped child. I knew she could use the help.

"Girl, now ain't the time for pride. We both know you can use it. Don't make little man suffer. Here…"

19

"But— " she started.

"But nothing." I shoved the money in her hand and balled a fist around it. "I'm honored to help you, Unique. In fact. I need a break. Will you cover me for about an hour?" I said with a smile.

Unique lit up. "Of course I will. Thank you, Jordyn. I owe you the world."

"Sure you do. Now, if you don't mind, lemme get outta here before it gets even crazier!"

"Sure. I got you, Jay-Jay. Anytime. You're the best, girl."

"Don't trip. Anytime."

And that's how it went. For two months, that was me and Unique's routine. Every Tuesday, before I slid out from alongside the bar, I'd reach into my pocket, pull out a wad of bills, and make my contributions towards little Trayvon's life. I love helping people. It gives me a sense of purpose. It's validating and comforting. I feel there's no greater joy in life than helping out a person in need.

On the ninth Tuesday, something fresh happened to me. Very fresh. I met a man. Not just any man though. *The* man. A very captivating and intriguing man; a man of impeccable poise and significant swagger; a fresh, suave, and debonair individual. The type of person you only meet once in life. The man of my dreams...

It happened just as I stepped from behind the bar to let Unique take over. I realized I forgot my phone and turned to get it. "Shoot," I said to myself. "Jordyn, you'd forget your own name if it wasn't tattooed inside your wrist."

I turned to get my phone, and that's when I ran into him. Literally.

"Watch it—Shit!" I looked down and a brown cognac stain was spreading against his white designer linen like a flesh eating disease. "OMG! I am so sorry. That's designer isn't it?" I asked stupidly. I already knew the answer. Louis Vuitton.

He looked down at the stain, then back into my eyes. He smiled. "Don't worry about it, beautiful. It's cool." His voice was smooth and mellow, like one of the Temptations or Five Heartbeats.

"Let me pay you," I forced out quickly.

"Don't worry about it," he said. "It's okay."

"No, it's not. Lemme pay, please. I'd feel better."

"Don't trip, Ma," he said smiling slyly. "It's only clothes."

I felt bad. Very bad. "You sure?" I asked.

"Of course I'm sure." He stuck out his hand. "Jordyn, right?"

I looked down at the Rolex on his wrist, and the huge diamond on his pinky. "How do you know my name?"

He nodded towards my wrist. "I heard you talkin' about being forgetful. Mind if I see it?"

I was so mesmerized by his beauty that I could've forgot my own birthday. "See-See what?"

He smiled that intoxicating smile. "The tattoo on your wrist. You are forgetful, huh?"

I was acting like a ditz. "Oh, I'm sorry…" I turned my wrist so that this handsome specimen could get a look.

"I like that," he admired. "So, you're into roses, huh?"

21

"Umm, well... I like flowers in general, but yes, red roses are my favorite."

"So, you wouldn't mind if I sent you any then?"

My face flushed red; red as the crimson rose on my inner-wrist. "Umm...well...you don't have to do that. I mean, I did ruin your linen."

"Oh, I didn't say I was sending them. I simply inquired if I could. To be honest, you should be sending me roses."

My mouth dropped. "What?"

"Yup. White roses for the white linen you ruined."

I blushed even harder.

"So that's how it is, huh?"

He nibbled his lower lip. My heart fluttered. I wanted to fall in his arms and tongue-kiss him right then. I don't think I'd ever been so physically attracted to a person in so short of time.

"That's right. Either you can send me roses, or take me out to dinner. Your pick."

I leaned back and analyzed him, giving him a slow and thorough once-over. *Light-brown skin, hazel eyes, low fade, icy-white teeth. Tempting... Definitely tempting.*

"Umm, okay," I said "But as long as you're not a serial killer. I don't do serial killers."

He laughed. "Serial killer?" A genuine laugh. "I may be many things, but a serial killer's not one of 'em."

"Good. Because I'm not trying to die."

"You won't die, Ms. Jordyn. I promise."

I stuck out my hand. "Good. Now what did you say your name was?"

"Cavalli…My name's Cavalli…"

Chapter Four

So, me and this Cavalli guy exchanged numbers with plans of hooking up the next day. God was I nervous! I mean, I'd been on dates before, even kissed a couple of guys afterwards, but none of them were like Cavalli. He was mature, polite, charismatic, gentle, and genuine.

Cavalli was a man's man, a man totally capable of chaperoning a beautiful young woman like myself around. But, there was one problem. I was the designated chaperone for the night. And I had the least possible clue as to where I'd take him. I hadn't been to many upscale restaurants in my day, and I definitely wasn't taking him anywhere shabby. Perception is everything in life, you know. How you're treated by a person is totally contingent on how you're perceived. Perception is reflection. That said, roadside diners and smorgasbords were totally out of the question. I had to put on for Cavalli. I had this weird feeling that he was gonna be my boo one day. And possibly my husband...

After a long deliberation period, I decided to have Cavalli meet me at Ruby Tuesdays. I know it wasn't much, but I liked Ruby's. They served good food there and were very homely. On top of that, the restaurant was only a mile or two from the club, so I could have my dinner and make it back to work before the rush.

I had a feeling that everything would be just fine.

I was already seated in a window-booth seat when Cavalli entered the restaurant. I half-expected him to be dressed down in, maybe denim shorts, a white t-shirt, and a pair of crisp Air Force Ones or something. But, to my surprise, Cavalli waltzed in wearing a dark brown Louis Vuitton linen short set, brown Louie loafers, and large designer frames to cover his brown luminous eyes. His caramel-drizzled lips were moist and delectable.

Oh, my God, I said to myself. *He is so fine! Be on your best behavior, Jordyn...   BE-HAVE!*

I waved my hand to get Cavalli's attention. "Hey, you!" Cavalli smiled and waved back. He said a few words to the hostess and began towards me. With his every step towards me the muscles between my legs began to tighten.

I shifted in my seat. *Oh, my God... He's definitely gonna be a problem. Definitely!*

"I see you came," Cavalli said smoothly and approached the booth. "To be honest, I thought you were gonna stand me up."

Stand you up? Boy you just don't know... I'm probably more ecstatic about being here than you are. You got a hold on me!

"Stand you up? What gave you the impression that I'd do something like that?"

I blushed. "I don't know." He really brought the schoolgirl outta me.

Cavalli took off his frames and sat them on the table next to his cell phone and car keys. "Women beautiful as you do weird stuff like that."

"Like what?"

"Sometimes you pretend to be interested in a cat like me. I get my hopes up high, and then, Bam! I get stood up."

I curled my lips. "You mean to tell me women stand you up. That's hard to believe."

Cavalli chuckled. "I didn't say *me*. I said guys *like* me. Fortunately, I don't have problems like that."

"Cocky *and* confident, huh?"

He licked his lips. "Everything in moderation. Everything in moderation… But, enough about me. I wanna know more about you. Tell me about yourself, Ms. Jordyn."

"You make me sound old when you say that."

"What? Ms. Jordyn. I apologize if I offended you. I just—"

"No. You didn't offend me. I have pretty thick skin."

Just as I spoke, a slim, red-faced waiter approached with ice water and menus. We placed our orders and Cavalli began probing.

"How old are you?"

"Nineteen. Well, I'll be nineteen in a couple of months. October to be exact. October ninth. And you?"

"Thirty-one. My birthday was a couple of weeks ago. Fourteenth of July."

I put my hand on his. "Aww. Happy belated birthday. Did you celebrate?"

He glanced down at my hand. "Yeah. I went to Africa."

"Africa-Africa?" I asked, astounded.

He smiled. "Yeah. Africa-Africa."

"Wow. You take pictures?"

"A couple. I'll e-mail you a few if you'd like."

"Sure. I'll give you the address before we leave."

Cavalli sipped his water. "Cool... What about your birthday tho'? Got anything planned?"

"I haven't really given it any thought. But, I'm a simple girl, so I'll probably just end up baking a cake and watching TV."

"That doesn't sound half-bad," he admitted. "Honestly, I would've rather sat at home and chilled myself. But..." he said with a sigh, "One of my business partners decided to schedule the trip without my knowledge. And if it's one thing I've learned about business and business partners, if you wanna stay on top of your game, appease."

"Sounds smart. And if you don't mind me asking, what kind of business do you do?"

"Mainly I flip house and cars, but I'll invest in pretty much anything worth a profit."

"So, you're pretty much just an investor, huh?"

"Pretty much."

"That has to be the best job ever. Nothing physical, just investing your money and watching it grow?" I looked up at the ceiling and shook my head. "Yup. Investing and watching my money grow."

"Well, it's not that simple. Sometimes it gets crazy."

"Oh, well now it sounds like *my* job."

Cavalli took another sip of water. "Speaking of your job, how'd you end up there. You'd think a woman beautiful as you would be somewhere more esteemed."

"My cousin owns the place. He conned me."

Cavalli laughed. "Conned you? You sure could've fooled me."

"And what's that supposed to mean? You know something I don't?" I was feeling more comfortable with every word.

"Nah, not really. Just seems like you like your job."

"I see someone's very observant, hm?" I squinted at him. "Sure you ain't a serial stalker after all?"

"Nah, I um… It's just… you look—"

"Go 'head. Spit it out," I teased. "Talk to me now."

He smiled. "You look…"

I cleared my throat and made a drumroll against the edge of the table. "Come on now. Don't choke up on me."

He smiled harder. "You look—you look dedicated," he said carefully.

I frowned and playfully slapped his hand. "Boy, you made me think you had something serious on me. Something devastating."

"Devastating? Why would you think that? You look like you're in your natural element when you're working."

I was unraveling into his arms. "Should've seen me at first. I was mortified!"

"Mortified? Why? Don't tell me you some type of closet drunk or something?"

"A closet dru—Boy you're crazy! No, I'm not a closet drunk. I just, well… I—I"

"Come on," he teased. "Your turn. Spit it out now."

I couldn't help but laugh. Cavalli had a serious sense of humor. It would've been easier to give up my virginity than avoid opening up to him. I could tell he was the one for me. I opened up too easily. Before I knew it I was sharing my entire life with him. My past experiences with men, dating, and clubs. Hell, I even told him about the couple of guys I kissed, and that was something I've never done. Tish didn't even know that. I was definitely comfortable with Cavalli. Very.

Our food arrived and in between bites I got to know him a bit more. I learned he had two brothers, one of whom were locked up for murder, the other happily married with kids. I learned Cavalli loved to travel, that he had a Cane Corso named Bully, and was head over heels for seafood. He graduated from high school, attended two years of college, had never been married, and eventually wanted kids. Thus far, Cavalli turned out to be a good catch. I really liked him. A lot. I liked the way he made direct eye contact with me when he spoke, the way his words were warm and soothing, and the fact that he could carry on a conversation without using slang or profanity. Cavalli was exceptional. He was definitely a man. I wondered if I could handle him?

I didn't want my date with Cavalli to ever end. But, I knew I had to get away. He was entirely too tempting. I quickly picked up the check and unzipped my bag. "I had a good time Cavalli. Thanks."

Cavalli took the check out of my hand. "I'll take care of it."

"But I thought this is where I paid you back for the linen I ruined?"

"How 'bout you pay for the next one."

I smiled. "And who said there'd be a next one, Mr. Cavalli?"

"Oh. So this was a date? For a second I was wonderin' if this was a business transaction. Where you repaid me for the linen you ruined."

"Okay, funny man. I see you got jokes."

"Always. Anything to see that beautiful smile."

I stood up and kissed Cavalli on the cheek.

"And what was that for?" he asked bashfully.

"The promise of a better date next time," I committed and walked confidently out of the restaurant.

Cavalli was tasty. Very, very tasty…

<u>Chapter Five</u>

Growing up, it seemed as if my beauty was a deterrent towards the opposite sex. My first boyfriend, Jaden, killed himself (over consumption of prescription meds), and the second, Malik, actually turned out to be gay. Now, I don't have any issues wit gays. Please don't get it misconstrued. But, to have your very first boyfriend kill himself, and the second one turn towards the same sex, it can be a heavy burden on you. It made me question my self-worth and inner beauty; ripped my self-esteem from its core and forced me back into the dungeon's shell I created when my parents died.

The unfortunate events of Jaden and Malik trashed me inside; to the point where I hadn't even thought of companionship or intimacy with another guy. And then Cavalli came. He was an amazing person; Smart, captivating, witty, very out-spoke, and oh-so charismatic. Cavalli helped me escape from the prison within. He made me feel worthy and just again. He let me know there was still a chance at finding a true love. He reintroduced me to life; rebirthed me. This was the new embryonic Jordyn Hayes. I was alive. Alive and ready to be loved!

Since the dinner at Ruby Tuesdays Cavalli and I had two more dates, and both were as pleasant as the first. We had chemistry. It's like we knew one another for years. This caused us to both let go and totally open up to one another. We shared more stories of our pasts, we ate good food, we laughed a lot, chilled, and then we had sex. Yes, you heard me. We had sex. Good, nasty, warm, sex. And it was amazing!

To be totally honest, I knew from the very moment I saw Cavalli that I was gonna give him some. He was so sexy; his cocoa brown eyes, his dark lips, smooth skin, and his awesome physique. So, I guess you can say sex with Cavalli was inevitable...

It happened on our third date. We were out bowling, having a good ol' time, when the final decision set in. I looked over at Cavalli, who'd just bowled a strike, and softened my eyes.

"I'm ready to leave," I said as kind as possible.

"Already?" he asked in a sort of dispirited tone. He was having fun.

"Yeah, I...I..."

"Don't tell me I bored you?" he said.

"No, no... I'm cool... I-I'm just—"

"Ready to go, huh?" Cavalli joked. "It's cool... Can't nobody in here out-bowl me anyway. Let's blow this joint!" he said with a laugh and threw his button up over his shoulder. To see him in those cargo shorts and wife beater did something to me.

Once we got outside to his car, I took control. "Your keys," I said with my extended hand. Cavalli gave me a weird look before cutting a glance over at his nearly hundred thousand dollar Porsche.

"Don't worry, I can drive."

He paused. "You sure?"

"Positively. Why else would I have these?" I said and held my driver's license in Cavalli's face.

Cavalli approached closely, so close that I could smell the Issey Miyake Cologne on his neck and wrist.

"Wouldn't be the first time I saw a fake I.D. You know they make those all the time."

I moved in closer, so that I was now only inches away from him. I could feel the warmth from his lips.

"What, you tryna call me a fake?" I said. Cavalli looked down into my eyes, then at my lips, as if he wanted to kiss them. He exhaled. I closed my eyes.

The breath from his caramel lips sent my entire insides ablaze.

My God, will you just kiss me! the voice inside me screamed.

Cavalli stepped back, shook his head, and instead of kissing me, handed me his keys.

"Here…you may have to adjust the seat a little bit, Shorty."

Cavalli was short, but I was shorter.

I fanned him off on my way to the driver's side. "Whatever. And you're not that tall either, Mr. Five-Five."

Cavalli smiled. "Yeah, well, I know someone who likes it," he added before plopping down into the passenger side of the expensive sports car.

Sure do, I thought. *A lot too! But I guess you already knew that, huh? So much for being inconspicuous, Ms. Jordyn…*

I pulled out of the bowling lane parking lot and drove idly around the city of Dayton, Ohio, while indulging Cavalli in more classic beginners-lover conversation. We rambled on and on, until finally, the final confirmation broke through to me.

I'm having sex with him, tonight. Yes. Tonight's the night! Tonight's the night you're gonna—wait! What did I just say? I know I didn't—

"Whoa!" Cavalli yelled and jerked the steering wheel to the right.

I screamed and recorrected, barely missing a parked SUV.

"Damn, you tryna kill me girl?"

"I'm—I'm so sorry," I stammered. "I was just—I was just..."

"You been sippin' on me girl?" Cavalli joked, making light of the situation.

"Of course not. I—I just, I'm sorry... I'm so sorry... I was just.. I just drifted off that's all. You wanna drive?"

"No, I'm cool..." he assured and readjusted himself in the seat. "I trust you. But, I would like to know what you were thinkin'. Of course, if you don't mind tellin' me?"

I blushed. "Why?"

"Because, it had to be juicy seeing you almost killed us."

"Juicy? And what exactly does that mean?"

"Juicy," he reiterated. "You never heard the term 'Juicy', as in 'Juicy Details'?"

I made a careful left hand turn on Wolf Road, near the old Pizza Hut.

"Yeah, I guess. But..."

"What. You're not that comfortable with me yet?"

"It's not that."

"You do remember our pact of honesty right?"

Cavalli had me on that one. On our second date, he and I promised to be 100% honest with one another. In fact, we made a pact to do our best at maintaining a firm level of communication with one another, no matter the subject or outcome.

"I'd rather keep it a secret," I said, keeping the playing field even. "You know, between me and the *inner Jordyn.*"

"The inner Jordyn?" he asked with his forehead wrinkled.

"Probably sounds crazy, huh?"

"Not really. I guess we all have our inner us. But, I thought we were buildin' somethin' here?"

"We are, but…"

How did I tell him? How could I look him in the eyes, tell him I wanted to have sex with him and expect him to respect me afterwards? And how would the words come out of my mouth? Would they pour forth freely? Or would I stammer about retardedly?

Just when I came to the conclusion that I'd never be able to not tell him, my apartment came into view. I pulled up out front, silenced the engine, and took a deep breath.

I shifted in the seat, so that I now faced Cavalli, and shook off the fear.

Here goes nothing, said the inner Jay-Jay.

"Cavalli," I said looking him directly in the eyes, "I like you. A lot. A very lot to be honest."

Cavalli smiled and touched my hand.

"I like you a lot too, Jordyn," he responded very smoothly. "What's up? Don't tell me this our last date?"

I took another deep breath. "Of course not. I just…"

"What? You can tell me."

"I can't do this," I said and nervously buried my face in my hands.

"It's cool, Jordyn. I promise. It's cool. Just be yourself. I told you that you can always be yourself with me. Always."

I took another deep breath. Then another, and another. I had to build up the courage.

"Okay," I said shaking my hands and fanning myself. "Here goes nothing... Ca-Cavalli, I, I..."

"Just be yourself, Jordyn. Be yourself."

Okay... Be yourself... Just be yourself, Jordyn... Another deep breath. *Here we go...*

"Cavalli," I said, after collecting myself, "I really like you. A lot. And the reason I wanted to leave the lanes so early is to get back here and have sex with you."

I immediately turned my face towards the driverside window.

Cavalli put his hand on my chin and lightly turned my head so that I faced him.

"You don't have to be ashamed. It's natural."

"I know. But I'm not like the other girls you've dated Cavalli."

"I know. That's why I like you so much."

"No, you don't understand. I know I told you about Jaden and Malik—and my fear of commitment—but I never told you I was a virgin."

Shockingly, Cavalli's facial expression didn't change. I expected his eyes to bulge out of his head and his mouth to drop on its hinge when I confessed that I was inexperienced, but, it didn't happen. In fact, Cavalli remained unfazed by my confession.

"I guess what I'm trying to say is… is, is… I don't want to bore you, Cavalli."

"Bore me? Are you serious? Jordyn you're the most interesting woman I've ever met. You could never bore me. And you don't have to be ashamed of your virginity. Most women can't say they held out 'til they were 15, let alone 18-19. And if they do, they're lying. I respect you, Jordyn. I really do. You're a beautiful person."

The corner of my lip turned up into a smile. "So, you're not turned off?"

"Turned off? If anything, I'm turned on!"

I laughed.

"I'm serious, Jordyn. Every man, at some point of their lives, fantasizes about meeting a beautiful young woman— a virgin—and being her all."

My face flushed. Cavalli had empowered me, made me feel honored.

The first thing I asked myself was whether or not sex with Cavalli would compromise our friendship. Would it sabotage my shot at getting the man of my dreams? Or, would it help solidify my position as Cavalli's wife? I asked a myself half dozen questions that night, and of them, the only thing that continuously materialized were the naked images of our bodies, intertwined in sexual bliss. I could hear the erotic moans of pleasure escaping from our moist mouths, the taste of Cavalli's caramel lips on mine. I guess my mind was already made, huh? I leaned over and planted a soft kiss on Cavalli's lips.

"I want you, Cavalli," I whispered. "I've wanted you from the very first time our eyes met. You're the man for me. I want you to be my all. Will you?"

Cavalli smiled. "Of course I will. Now, which apartment is yours," he said with a smile.

<u>Chapter Six</u>

As soon as my front door was closed, Cavalli and I were at it.

"Slow down," he said softly, as I straddled him fully clothed on the couch, sucking at his lips and rubbing his head.

"I'm sorry," I apologized.

"You don't have to be sorry, Jordyn," Cavalli said before kissing me gently on the nape of my neck. "I just want this to last. Now, if you will... lead me to your lair."

I smiled and led Cavalli by the hand to my bedroom.

Once we entered my bedroom, Cavalli led me to the foot of my bed.

"Sit down," he gestured and began undressing me. "Just relax..." he coaxed. "Let daddy take care of you."

Cavalli removed all of my clothing and began running his hands sensually all over my body, showing special interest in my neck, shoulders, between and around my breast, my stomach, down my thighs, and the small stretch of skin behind my knees, and then down onto my feet.

He lifted my foot and gently kissed my toes. "You're so beautiful, Jordyn. I wanna taste you. Can I taste you?"

I chewed at the bottom of my lip, approvingly. Cavalli then parted my legs and slowly began to lick between them.

"Oh my God," I moaned and covered my head with a pillow. Cavalli was good with his tongue. The way he maneuvered it back and forth and up and down against my clitoris drove me crazy. It sent a sensation throughout my body so intense that I felt as if I were going to explode in bliss.

That has to be an orgasm building... I thought. *Oh my God! I don't— I don't—I don't think I can handle this...*

"Oh my God!" I moaned louder. "Oh my God!"

"You like that?" Cavalli whispered in between firm flicks of his tongue. "You like that? Don't be shy... Tell me you like it? You like it?"

"I like it," I cooed. "Yes. I like it."

Cavalli flicked his tongue a click faster and slid his finger inside. I jumped.

He hesitated. "You okay? Want me to stop?"

"No. Don't stop. Please, don't stop."

Cavalli slid his finger back inside of me and nibbled my clit until my body pulsated. "Oh, Cavalli—Oh yes...Yes...Yes!"

"You like that? You like it?" he asked with his mouth on me.

"I like it. Yes. Yes, yes... Yes!"

"Yes what? Yes what?"

I gasped. "Yes, I like it," I confessed, and I leaned up to watch Cavalli do his thing. "Yes, I like it! God! Yes! I like it! Yes, yes, yes! Oh I like it! I like—Ahhhh!" I screamed as my first orgasm ever passed through my body. I grabbed Cavalli's head with both hands and slammed my head back on the bed.

"Oh my—oh my—aaaaahhhhh!" I shrieked as the orgasm rocked my body. "Oh my God! Oh my—aaaahhhhh!" I yelled as the second orgasm approached. "Ah—Oh my God! Aaaaaahhh!"

I couldn't take it anymore. I back-pedaled to free myself from Cavalli's skillful tongue. "No! Please. No more. No more!"

Cavalli laughed. "What?" he asked facetiously. "You don't like that?"

"Boy you—Huh-hn. No! Keep that thing away from me."

Cavalli stood and dropped his pants. "What about this?"

I looked down at the pulsating mass of caramel and spread my legs.

I always wondered what it'd feel like? You know, if it'd be a subtle pain, or a pain so tormenting that I wished I was dead. I wondered how long the pain would last, and if it'd be better to be with a large man or a small man for my first time.

These were the questions that filled my mind. But, Cavalli answered all them for me. He gently parted my legs and guided the tip of his thickness inside of me. I winced at first but the pain was quick. Cavalli was patient. He inched himself inside of me slowly, fulfilling me with his love inch by inch by inch.

"Oh, yes," I moaned in his ear and pulled him closer. "Ooooh, yes... Yes. Yes."

"Was it worth the wait?" Cavalli whispered in my ear, as he stroked slowly up and down.

"Every bit of it."

Sex with Cavalli was beautiful. Very, very beautiful.

I was hooked.

<u>**Chapter Seven**</u>

Cavalli had me by the soul! No other human being on the face of this earth had ever affected me the way he did. He had me all messed up. I'm talking both mentally and physically. We'd only been dating for a total of six months and he already had me under his spell. All that man had to do was run his hot pink tongue over his thick brown lips and I was literally stripping down out of my clothes. I had it bad. I was whipped!

So, yes, I'd officially been wooed and subdued. But the greatest part was I liked it. No. Let me rephrase that: I loved it! Cavalli was the handsome and talented charmer, and I, the sexy mistress under his spell.

Around our six month anniversary, Cavalli led me a little further into his world. Up until that point I'd only been made privy to join him at his loft. It was a nice place, real nice to be honest. But I knew it wasn't his home. There was a strong look of separateness to him when we were there. Almost as if it were a secret bachelor pad or even a close friend's place. There were no pictures of him with friends or family, and there was no sign of best friend and pet, Bully, the Cane Corso.

I was fully aware that there was a large part of Cavalli's life that I wasn't a part of, but, should I have been mad at him for not inviting me in? I mean, we were just friends, right? I did have my own place, and he did help out with bills, on top of ravishing me with all types of lavish gifts and things. But should I have wanted more? Should I have sought commitment from Cavalli? Should I have questioned our relationship and his separateness? Or, should I have just been content with what I had? I'm guessing only a fool would ask for more, huh?

*   *   *

I was curled up on my chaise eating ice cream and watching television when my phone rang. It was Cavalli. Calling for the fourth time in three hours. And each time his questions grew more and more obvious. He was planning something, but didn't want me to know what. He wanted to know my exact whereabouts, my plans for the day, and if I'd be free.

I figured this call would be the same.

"Hey Babe." That was me.

"What up sweetheart. So, did you decide if you were gonna be free tonight?"

He knew I was. But I played along anyway. "For you? Of course I will."

"Can you be ready in, umm... say, an hour?"

"Umm..." I stalled playfully, to add to the thrill of our little game of cat and mouse. "I think so. Anything specific you need me to wear? Or don't wear for that matter."

"I like that," he said coolly. "Yeah... Wear that Gucci dress I brought you a couple months ago. The black one."

"Red Bottoms, too?"

"Of Course."

"Any preference for my hair? Up, down, ponytail?"

"Good question..." he said and clicked his tongue. "Ponytail. You know I'm a sucker for ponytails." And that he was. He liked it when I pulled my long black hair back into a ponytail just before sex. He'd wrap the length of it around his fist and pull it gently as he took me from behind. "Okay, Daddy," I said in my sexy voice. "Gucci dress, red bottoms, and ponytail it is."

"Cool. See you in an hour."

"Okay."

I smiled a wide smile and clicked off my television set. Forty minutes later I was showered, dressed, and had my hair pulled back in ponytail.

When the doorbell rang I was checking my lip-gloss in the mirror behind the front door. I didn't even bother checking the peephole. I already knew who it was. I grabbed my black Gucci clutch (that Cavalli bought as well) and swung open the door. "Hey, baby," I said to Cavalli who was standing in the doorway wearing a dark-blue blazer, white and blue button-up, denim jeans, and all white Air Force One's. His navy-blue and white New York Yankee fitted-cap added just the right amount of swagger to his ensemble. Cavalli stepped in the doorway and hugged me, sniffed my neck. "Damn. You smell like heaven. Turn around... Lemme see you. Um!"

I did a little spin and cocked my leg to the side to flaunt my expensive heels. "You like?" I asked approvingly.

"Of course I do. I know what my baby look good in." My face flushed. I batted my eyes and smiled.

"C'mon, you ready?" he asked.

I pulled my door up and locked it behind me.

After about five minutes on the road, I asked, "So, where we going tonight? Let me guess, Delish? Or, wait. It's Sunday night. Friedman's?"

Cavalli grabbed my hand and smiled. "It's a secret. But I promise you'll like it."

"You promise?"

"I promise," he assured and planted a kiss on my hand.

We took I-75 north until we reached the Third Street Downtown Dayton exit. As soon as we entered downtown the smell of fresh bread and pastries infiltrated Cavalli's ventilation system, suddenly creating a craving for a croissant with cream cheese or a salmon croquette on sourdough bread. I was a little petite woman, but I could throw down. In fact, as I sat on the passenger side of Cavalli's Mercedes, I secretly wished there was food somewhere in this equation.

As we rounded the corner near Monument boulevard and the Green Bridge, Cavalli put his hand over my face. "Close your eyes," he said quickly. "Hurry, I don't want you to see!"

"You have to be kidding me."

"No, I'm serious," he said. "Now close your eyes before you ruin the surprise."

I sighed and obeyed Cavalli's wish. I felt the car pull right, then left, and another soft right.

"Okay. Now you can open." When I parted my eyes, I half expected to see a pair of juggling elephants or a pack of red-booty dancing baboons. But, all there was was a brick wall with a small sign attached to it that read: Reserved for owner.

"Cavalli, what are you up to?"

Cavalli put a finger up to my lip. "Shh. Just follow me."

I grabbed my clutch and joined Cavalli outside the car. There were several people exiting their vehicles, mainly in couples, all walking in the direction we were. Cavalli spoke, shook a couple of hands, and we walked quietly towards the front of the building.

I immediately took notice that all the guests were dressed casual. The men wore either suits or blazers, with jeans or slacks, while the women adorned designer dresses and heels, or glitzy shirts and leggings. Wherever we were going, Cavalli and I were gonna fit in just fine.

When we rounded the corner on Kay Street a line of maybe thirty or forty people protruded from the front door of this unfamiliar establishment. Cavalli gently slid his arm around my waist and escorted me around the waiting patrons. He smiled and, forever the gentleman, shook more hands and waved. As we approached the main entrance of the building, Cavalli slowed his stride and turned to me. "Ready for the surprise?" he asked, and without granting me a single solitary second of acceptance, he pointed at the brick facade. "Congratulations," he said and pulled at a thick red cord connected to a white tarp. "You're officially a business owner!" The white tarp fell from the brick facade revealing a luminous neon purple sign that read *Jordyn's*.

"I can't... Wait... What?" I was at a lost for words. Not only did he say it was mines, but he also named it after me. "This has to be a joke?"

Cavalli kissed me lightly on the cheek. "Of course not. It's yours, baby. Hope you don't mind me using your real name. I started to use Jay-Jay, but I figured you'd like Jordyn's better. It has a more classier ring to it."

I couldn't speak. Temporary paralysis sat in and I found myself stuttering. I was in a state of shock and awe. I was confused.

"You alright baby?"

"Yeah, I just... I'm... I'm just stunned. Nobody has ever done anything like this for me. I don't... I don't know what to say."

"Don't say anything. I already know how you feel. Just continue loving me and—"

"Mr. Cavalli," a dark-skinned man wearing a tight–black shirt and earpiece cut in. "Sorry to interfere," he said at Cavalli's shoulder.

"No problem. We on schedule?" Cavalli questioned.

"So far 200 of your 240 guests have arrived and been seated." He bent his head to see around us and furthered with, "the other 40-or-so appear to be in line."

"Good. See to it that they all get in and get seated as promptly as possible. These are my closest friends and family here, Maurice. Treat 'em good."

"Most certainly," the big black man in black said obediently.

Maurice unclasped the velvet rope and let us pass. "Next."

The inside of Jordyn's was amazing! The walls were upholstered with a stunning black velvety fabric, and the floors were made up of a brown and black marble design. The seating arrangements consisted of three dozen comfortable booths and tables that were consistent with the natural hue of the walls and flooring, and the entire upper half of the building was the dance floor, which was awesomely created to depict a scene of West African colonization; two six-foot-tall wooden African Warrior statues flanked either side of the black and brown checkered glossy dance floor, while another guard stood watch over a glass display case that stocked the building's fair array of beverages. (There was a small amount of alcoholic beverages held against the decorative wall-shelf behind the glass display case, but the main source of goods were stored inside: exquisite blends of imported teas, coffees, and creamers; rare cappuccinos, nuts, muffins, and exotic cakes and cookies.)

Off to the side of the glass display case were four book stands and a magazine stand—which offered both rare and well-sought African Books and magazines—and next to it was a fragrance case that stored fragrances as modern as Roc 98, Usher, and Sean John, and as legendary as Myrrh, Sandalwood, Juniper, and Frankincense. Jordyn's was definitely more different than anything I'd ever seen, and I was truly honored to be a part of it.

Cavalli had me take a seat front center the room, at an oval table with wine-scented candles and sparkling water waiting, and he took the floor. "Excuse me everyone," he said into the mic. "Excuse me..."

When everyone turned to face him he took a sip of his water and addressed the crowd. "First off, I must say thank you to this beautiful crowd for coming out... I truly appreciate having you all. You know we got some great spots in the city. We got Vinney's, Friedman's, Delish, Aphrodisiac, The Vault, even Red Light District. But ain't no spots like this. Ain't nowhere for us black people to go and get enlightened while we have a good time, nowhere to sit back and relax and gauge the inner growth and spirituality of one another while we embrace the heritage and long lost traditions of our ancestors... Nowhere to find that vintage Leslie Allen book, or pick up a copy of the Lost Words and Essays of The Honorable Elijah Muhammad." Cavalli fanned his hand over the room and continued. "Well, you have that here. We got poetry slams set up for Sundays, candle-making evenings and wine tasting for the ladies on Wednesday's and Thursday's, and the first Tuesday of every month we'll be hosting small business classes with our local SBA. It's all about evolution..."

Cavalli took another sip of water and continued. "...Which brings me to *my* future... For those of you who haven't met her yet, this is Ms. Jordyn Hayes, my beautiful muse."

I waved to the crowd and wondered if I should stand. Probably not. I was so embarrassed that I was sure to do something foolish, like tip back onto the table or rip the tablecloth off when I stood. So I settled with a smile and a wave.

"Since the very day I met this woman, my life hasn't been the same. She brought so much light and purpose to my life it's crazy. Jordyn made me just wanna just flap my wings and fly off." He looked at me and smiled. "Hopefully... God willing... she'll let me fly off with her... Before I keep going on though, I wanna share this story that my grandfather told me when I was about fifteen years old... It's about an old man and a wooden box. This old man, he was a master carpenter. A man more talented with his hands than anybody in his entire town. A man who'd spent most of his years in total devotion to perfecting his creation, a sleek box designed to house all his fears, shortcomings, and mishaps.

This old man worked endlessly at modifying and reconstructing his prized work. The only problem was, no matter how incessantly he worked, he could never manage perfection...

For those of you who don't know the story, this box would never succumb to his continuous alterings, upgrades, and modifications. Why? Because, what he didn't know, he, nor his box—symbolic of his life—would ever be complete, no matter how hard he tried... For each of his downfalls in life, for every inadequacy or failure he suffered, he altered the box, thus consuming his entire life with his work. Every day, every minute, every hour, he worked. In the end, the master carpenter worried himself to death. He put so much time and effort into his job that he literally worked himself to death. And you know what they buried him in? You guessed it, his precious box."

Cavalli looked at me with a deep intensity in his eyes. He licked his lips then focused back on the crowd behind me. "My grandfather made sure I understood the principles of life, love, and relationships before he died. And that's why I'm here today..."

Cavalli stepped closer to me and stuck his hand in his pant pocket. "I can't let this opportunity pass, Jordyn," he said as he pulled out the red box. "Will you do me the honor of being my wife?" My heart stopped. No, I'm serious. My heart skipped a couple beats. I put my hand over my mouth and blinked my eyes to focus in on the monstrous diamond peeking out the box. He was serious. Very serious. So serious that I couldn't breathe. I grabbed the sparkling water from the table before me and took a large, unlady-like gulp.

Cavalli removed the diamond ring from its prison and scooted closer to me. "Will you?" he asked, his big brown eyes begging of me.

Tears rushed down the hot canvas of my flushed cheeks and I lost my hearing. My heart pounded in my chest like a bass drum, and my fingers went numb. My tongue swelled in my mouth like a water balloon, and more tears poured out.

I was ecstatic and embarrassed.

How could he ask me to marry him in front of all these people? How could he do something like that? How could he up and—

Wait! He asked me to marry him? He asked *me* to marry him? The man whom I'd fallen so deeply in love with. The very individual who, since the day I met him all I wanted to do was please him, make him smile, make him feel like a man. This was him. Kneeling before me with a huge diamond in his hand, asking me to be his for the remainder of our lives.

Why did I stall? All Cavalli wanted to do was love me. And who was I trying to kid? I knew full and well that all I wanted was to be his wife. God had sent me a man in the righteous image of my father, and I couldn't let it pass. So, yes, I'd marry him. Yes! Yes, yes, yes, yes! Yes to the man who cared so much about me that he not only purchased a business in my name, but also named it after me. Yes to the man who wanted to have and to hold me, through sickness and health, 'till death do us part. Yes! Yes to the man who accepted me for exactly who I was, and didn't desert me like the other men of my past, Malik and Jaden. No. Not like them. This was my knight and shining armor. This was *my* African Warrior, my fighter and keeper of endless love and compassion. This was my man, my investor of imported and exported goods, who wanted nothing more in life than to take care of me and see me happy; to sit me up on the hill with the big house, the white picket fence, and the beautiful kids. This was my supper hubby! Yes, I'd marry him. Yes!

I looked to Cavalli and chewed at my bottom lip. "Yes... Yes, I'll marry you, Cavalli. Yes, Yes, Yes!"

Cavalli slid the ring down my finger and wiped a tear from my face. "I love you, Jordyn. Always and forever."
"Always and forever," I repeated to him. "Always and forever..."

Chapter Eight

Immediately after Cavalli proposed to me, he moved me out of my humble one bedroom apartment and into his glorious 7 bedroom, 6 bathroom mini-mansion, located in the gated community of Ashton Village. His home was absolutely stunning! Twenty-foot vaulted ceilings, a winding staircase that overlooked a vast expansive living quarters, an Olympic-styled swimming pool, six car garage—that held two late model Porsches, two motorcycles, a Cadillac SUV, a 3-wheel Spider, and my brand new retractable hardtop Mercedes Benz— a full-court basketball court, personal gym and theater, and not one, but three Jacuzzis.

Cavalli's home was absolutely awesome. Tasteful paintings and black chandeliers covered every inch of the 4900 square foot home, while the latest in appliances and technology updated and completely advanced the home, qualifying it for best styled/ most technologically equipped in Architectural Digest. But I didn't quite know if I'd be comfortable there. To be honest, I was a little out of my element. I'd never been in a house so luxurious and well kempt. And I believe Cavalli knew this. This is why he only invited me to his apartment at first. We were still early in our relationship, and I think he knew I would've gone in to shock seeing all that stuff. But getting to know him first made a big difference. It helped me see Cavalli for who he truly was. All the glitz and glamour didn't cause me to see him as arrogant, boastful, or pretentious. Instead it allowed me to see Cavalli for the humble, unassuming, free-giving man he was. A man who didn't mind sharing his wealth with other people. The type of person who took more pleasure in giving than receiving. The type of person who'd rather donate millions anonymously, rather than donate thousands on camera in front of a live audience. Cavalli was rich and rare and I loved him.

Cavalli always seemed to know how to make me happy. For instance, as if moving me out of my apartment and into the biggest home I've ever stepped foot in wasn't enough, as soon as I entered the master bedroom for the very first time, I was presented with a brand new high-end wardrobe. The closet was so big I could've lived in there. He must've spent thousands stock-piling it. "Wow," I said running my hands over the expensive garments. "You must've paid a fortune for all this stuff."

Cavalli stepped closer and took my hands into his. "As long as you're with me, Jordyn, you don't ever have to worry about money. Ever. You're my fiancée, soon to be my wife. What's mines is yours. You see it, want it, buy it. Flat out. You're my Queen. You hear me, Jordyn? You hear me?"

I heard him. Loud and clearly. But I was too turned on to function normally. My vagina was too warm to think straight.

I dropped down on my knees in front of him.

"Wait... What you doin'?" he questioned, as I shushed him and unclasped his belt buckle. I pulled him out and moaned at the sight.

I had never performed oral before. Not once. Not even with all of the sex Cavalli and I were having. I still hadn't worked my way up to it (no pun intended). But I admit that I did feel kind of obliged every time Cavalli performed it on me. (Which was a lot!) Every time he parted my legs and tasted me, sapped my sweet nectar, I wanted to reciprocate the gesture. The only problem was, I was afraid. I didn't know if I'd be good, or if I'd totally suck(Again, no pun). So, I started doing research. I searched the internet, reading tips from porn stars and studying their techniques. I practiced on popsicles and blowpops until I was sure I'd give Cavalli a good blowjob. And then I did it.

I let Cavalli's pants fall to the floor and eyed his penis. It wasn't the biggest I'd seen—of course most porn stars are above average—but it wasn't small by far. I wrapped my hands around it and squeezed it a bit, watched it grow underneath my touch, getting larger and larger by the pulse. Before long, the tip was literally poking out from the top of my hand like a brown snake from its home. I stuck the tip of my tongue out and tasted him. I opened my mouth wide and put the entire tip in. Cavalli moaned and dropped his head back. Good sign. I twirled my tongue around and Cavalli moaned louder. Definitely on to something now. So I began bobbing my head up and down, back and forth, like I'd seen on the videos. Cavalli took obvious pleasure to this. His body jerked and he rubbed the side of my head and face. I pulled him out of my mouth and gently slapped him against face like I'd seen Pinky do, and, whoa did that drive him wild! He gasped and stumbled back towards the bed. But I wasn't letting him get away that easily. Not after what he'd done to me with his tongue. I wanted to break him the way he'd broke me. So I bobbed and sucked and slobbered on Cavalli until he couldn't take it any longer. He grew bigger and bigger in my mouth and pulsated like a vein in a weight-lifter's forehead. I still didn't give in. I kept at it with persistency and determination, and then, it finally happened. "Oh my—oh my God!" he hissed. "I'm 'bout'ta cum! I'm 'bout'ta," and he pulled out, spraying my face, neck, and cleavage with his thick creamy love juice, leaving me glossy, glazed, and more turned on than ever. I wanted Cavalli. I wanted Cavalli *in* me. The warmth and texture of Cavalli's cum on me had me so wet that I could feel the drip-drop from my vagina in my panties.

Cavalli fell back on the bed and held his head in his hands with a pained look on his face. I stepped out of my panties. "I'm soaked," I said, looking down at my vagina. "God, I never knew I could get so wet."

My words were like an aphrodisiac to Cavalli. His penis rose from the side of his leg as if it were being pulled by a string. It teetered left, then right, and throbbed out for my touch. "Come here," He said softly. "Lemme see how wet you really are..."

I *fucked* Cavalli that day. I mean, I really *fucked* him. It wasn't like the other times when we were having sex. I was in total control this day. I rode him forwards, backwards, even made him take me from behind. I came three times before Cavalli got off his second, and two more times after that (via his tongue). I wanted to go another round, fucking him some more, but Cavalli had an important meeting and I didn't want him to reschedule.

Cavalli had started something with me. Something I really hoped he could finish...

*   *   *

By the third week out to Cavalli's I was totally at home. I now moved with an air of elegance and opulence about myself. One that said I was born for this life. I entertained our guests like a true Queen, getting them anything and everything they requested or desired. And I made my man very happy doing so. He showered with more high-end gifts, more designer handbags, more expensive heels, and more extravagant jewelry. And I in turn, treated Cavalli to more exhilarating and tantalizing sex. Cavalli was the best!

<u>Chapter Nine</u>

I was sitting at the dining room table overlooking purchase orders for Jordyn's when Cavalli walked in. I looked up from my laptop and smiled. "Hey, Babe," I said and quickly cut my eyes back down to the ten inch computer screen. I had work to do. "Lunch is in the mic, baked you some chicken and mac 'n' cheese. I'll start dinner in a couple of hours, when I finish here."
Cavalli walked up and planted a kiss on the top of my head. "Thanks. Che come by yet?" Che was one of Cavalli's closest friends/business associates.
"Um, yeah. He left his car in the garage. Said something about you dropping it off to the shop. The keys are on the mantel."
Cavalli turned his eyes in the general direction of the mantel. "He say anything else?"
I typed a couple more characters. "Umm… Nope. Except to tell you your old driver wasn't able to make it. Whatever that means."
Cavalli paused, briefly. "Hm." He pulled out his cell and typed a quick text. "So, what you doin'?" he asked and snuggled me from behind.
"Nothin' much. Just going over these purchase orders."
"Why? What's wrong?" Cavalli questioned defensively.
"It's just… Well, it seems we're over-stocked."
I could feel Cavalli's eyes on me. "Over-stocked? Where?"
I pointed at the screen. "See? Here, here, and there. It seems as if our entire Afghanistan order was doubled."

"Afghanistan huh?"

"Yeah. Afghanistan. Where we get our coffee and nuts from. Funny isn't it? We only ordered a total of sixteen boxes, but we received and were charged for thirty-two boxes."

Cavalli shut the laptop. "You worry too much," he said. " Besides, isn't that Jessica's job anyway? Since when did you become an accountant?" he asked jokingly. But I wasn't laughing. This was my integrity and my name on the line. I couldn't fail.

"Ever since I became a business owner," I answered half seriously.

"You worry too much. You need to relax. Come here..." he said and pulled me to my feet. He wrapped his arms around me and kissed me on the forehead. "Let homegirl take care of that. She's the best at what she does."

"But—"

"But, nothing. Trust me, if it's somethin' erroneous in the order she'll find it. All you need to worry about is maintain' this beautiful body of yours." Cavalli smacked me lightly on the butt and kissed my bottom lip.

"I'm getting fat as it is. I think I need to lose some weight." I spinned around so he could view my ass. "You think I'm gaining weight?"

Cavalli leaned back and held his finger out at me. "No," he said as if I were a child. "Absolutely not. You're getting thick, and I love it. Don't nobody wanna be shackin' up wit a bag of bones. That's ass right there. A big ol' juicy ass!" he said and smacked my butt again, making it jiggle.

"Whatever," I said and sat back down. "I'm fat."

"No you're not. But you do need to get out more."

"And go where? Remy and Tish are always on some romantic date, and Unique and Michelle are always busy down at the club."

"What about Arryn, Tyrone's wife?"

"Those are *your* friends, not mines."

"But I thought you liked Arryn?"

"No, I don't. She's not my type. And besides, she doesn't even like me."

Cavalli chuckled. "And where did that come from? I thought you two were cool."

"Nope," I said plainly. "She's jealous of me. Very jealous. And I think she likes you."

Cavalli laughed. "And what brought you to that brilliant conclusion, Ms. Einstein?"

"It's all in her smile."

"Her, what?"

"You heard me. Her smile."

"Girl, you're crazy."

"No, I'm not. I see the truth in her eyes every time she flashes that plastic-ass smile at me. She thinks I'm stupid because I'm a little younger. Well, I'm not. And if she thinks she's getting my man, she has another thing coming. I'll backhand that hoe."

Cavalli laughed and shook his head. But not the type of shake that said I was lying, I wouldn't do it. The type that said you're crazy.

"Well, you wanna go shopping?" he asked, knowing full well a day of shopping could always brighten a girl's day up.

I batted my eyelashes. "I guess. I did see a few things in Macy's I wanted. You coming with me though? You know I hate shopping by myself."

Cavalli planted another soft kiss on my forehead. "I would if I could. But you know I got that one thing to do with the realtor, remember?"

"What one thing?"

"Remember when I told you about the properties I sold last week? The ones down in Atlanta? Well, I gotta go downtown with the realtor to sign a few more papers. He flew in this morning."

I pouted like a spoiled child. "And why can't the realtor sign them for you?"

"Um, probably because it's a criminal offense to forge someone's signature."

"I'm pretty sure it's nothing he hasn't done before."

"Probably not. But, I bet it's something he doesn't like to do on the regular." I pouted. "Don't do that, Jordyn. You know I hate to see you like that. Here…" he said and pulled out his wallet and handed me his Black Card. "Get whatever you want. Whatever"

I pouted again. "But I want you."

"And you'll get me, tonight. But I gotta take care of this business. It's very important. Tonight. You got my word."

"You promise?"

"I promise. I'll even make reservations at that restaurant you like on my way to the signing."

I looked up into Cavalli's eyes. I hated the hold he had on me. He was so charismatic and alluring. "Okay," I said and took the credit card between my fingertips. "But you better not stand me up."

"I won't. I gave you my word."

I leaned up and kissed him on the lips. "Love you."

"Love you, too." Cavalli turned and started for the front door. "Oh," he said with a shake of his finger. "I forgot something. You mind doin' me a favor?" he asked.

I shrugged my shoulders. "I don't care. No—wait. Does it include me on top of you, or somewhere in between. If not it's a big N-O."

"Girl, you're crazy for real," he admitted smiling. "But, seriously, would you do me a favor?"

"Does it include me on top of you, or somewhere between? If so, yes. If not, no."

He smiled again, but quickly removed it, to show me he was serious. "Of course."

"Deal," I said and shook his hand. "Now, what you need me to do?"

"Che's Mercedes… You feel like droppin' it off for me? The address is already in the GPS, and there's a rental waiting on you. A red Ford Focus."

I didn't give it any thought. "That's it? That's the big favor? Of course I'll do it. Wait... It will make it, won't it?"

"Of course it will. And if for any reason it doesn't, use the emergency service center I put in your phone."

"Gotcha."

"Cool," he said and turned towards the door. "Oh, and the keys to the Ford'll be in the ignition. It's already gas in there too."

"Alright-y. Consider it done."

"Thanks again, baby. I'll text you the time for dinner so you're ready."

"M-kay. Love you."

"Love you too…"

I left exactly twenty minutes later. And the white Mercedes drove perfectly. There were no crazy smells emanating from the engine, or flashing warning lights blinking on the dash. Everything seemed to be a-okay.

I was approximately six miles from my destination, just getting off the I-75 conjuncture ramp, when I heard a loud boom and felt the steering wheel jerk violently to the left. I screamed and gripped the wheel, maneuvering the high-priced sedan to the right side of the road. I got out and found the right front tire blown out. "Shit! Just my fucking luck!" I was never a fan of profanity, but situations like that could always bring a colorful word or two out of me. I pulled out my phone and called the roadside service people Cavalli had added to my list of contacts. They picked up on the second ring. "Tim's Roadside Assistance, how may I help you?"

"Yes, I had a blowout, and I need assistance, like, now."

"And what is your carrier number, Ma'am?"

"Carrier, what?" I asked looking up at the blistering hot sun. It was scorching outside.

"The locator number on the card we provided you."

"Well, my fiancé put your number in my phone as a emergency contact. I don't have any card."

"Oh. Okay. Well, what's your husband's name?"

"Cavalli. Cavalli Mar—"

"No. No last names, Ma'am."

"No last—well, okay then. No last names. His name is Cavalli… CA-VA-LLI." I immediately heard computer keys being typed. "Okay," the operator said. "Someone's in route. Stay off the road, and if any other assistance crews or authority figures show up, just tell 'em you're waiting on Triple A."

"Oh, okay. Thanks."

"No problem. We aim to serve…"

While I stood outside the passenger side of the Mercedes waiting for roadside assistance, I began to work up a light sweat. My shirt began sticking to the small of my back giving me a sticky feeling I definitely wouldn't want to take with me shopping, so I took to the trunk, about to remove the spare so that I was ready for Tim's Roadside Assistance—or Triple A, or whoever—when they showed up. I used the small black box on the keychain to pop the trunk. A black SUV passed just as I pressed the button and the driver kinda eyed me suspiciously. I looked the middle aged African-American man in his eyes as he came to a stop at the end of the off ramp. He had bushy eye-brows, a small afro, and a weasely nose. Creepy, I said to myself. *Ugh,* I shuddered and looked into the trunk. A black tarp covered the entire canvas of the trunk. I pulled it back, half-prepared to see old gym clothes or something, but what I saw appalled me. "Oh-my-god," I said and covered my mouth. I couldn't believe my eyes. Standing before me, the trunk was filled to the hilt with contraband. And I mean filled! From the left to the right—back to front—was either guns, drugs, or cash. I couldn't believe it.

"What the fuck!" I said aloud. "Cavalli, I'm gonna kill—" and just as I was about call him and scream the nastiest, filthiest, expletives in his ear, the roadside assistance truck showed up. I was really in trouble now.

When the tire blew, I managed to maneuver the Mercedes to the far end of the conjuncture ramp, the closest to the stop sign at the four-way stop I could get. Now I was wishing I hadn't. I wished I'd pulled over somewhere where he'd had a harder time reaching me. Somewhere where I could've pulled the spare out before he could get a glimpse of the contents of Che's trunk.

The blue van decorated with Tim's Roadside Assistance number and logo pulled up nose-to-nose to the Mercedes. I panicked and hurried at the spare. It was buried deep, deep underneath the contraband. I didn't know if I'd make it. My freshly manicured nails broke and cracked as blood shot from my cuticles. I had to hurry. "Ms. Hayes?" he called out. "Ms. Hayes?" *How does he know my name?* I thought. *And how the hell did he get to me so quickly? I didn't even tell him where I—* "Ms. Hayes?" he called out again.

By now he was at the nose of the Mercedes.

"Ms. Hayes," he called out for the third time, just as I grabbed the spare and lifted it out the trunk. "Ms. Hayes?"

Shit, shit, shit!

"Ms. Hayes? Ms. Hay—? Oh, there you are," he said and eyed my oily shirt. "You do know you could've waited, right? It's my job to get you all fixed up and back on the road."

I stood there stunned, the spare tire against my designer pant leg, panting. "Oh, it's okay. I didn't—I didn't know how long you'd be and, and..."

"Here, let me get that," he said and took the tire from me. "No woman as beautiful as you are should ever be dealing with something as filthy as this." He picked up the tire and laid it against his blue coverall. He was thin and brown-skinned but he seemed to have a ton of muscles underneath there. Thank God he wasn't strong *and* nosy. Only God knows what would've happened then.

Dwight. (That was his name.) He had me back on the road in a little under ten minutes. I waved a fake wave, sighed, and pulled off before he was even back in his van.

I was seconds away from calling Cavalli and screaming WTF! into the phone, but I was so upset and heartbroken that I couldn't bring myself to do it. I didn't even want to talk to him at the moment. I couldn't. And besides, I wanted to look him in the eye when I checked him. I wanted to gauge the honesty and sincerity in his eyes before I left him. Yes, he was very persuasive, but there's no way he was gonna talk his way outta this one. No way. In fact, there'd be no more of me and Cavalli once I saw him, and this I was sure of. Positive.

When I pulled up at the destination given to me by the GPS, I looked on in awe. It looked more like an empty warehouse than that of an auto-mechanic's shop. There were old steel drums and all types and sorts of debris littered about, and everywhere you looked, it seemed to be some form of rusty metal protruding. A wooden door sat just beyond a steel ramp leading into the old debilitated building, and judging by its newness, either at that very point, or some time not long ago, that building was being occupied. I wasn't sticking around to find out by whom though. I pulled the Mercedes next to the gleaming red Ford Focus, silenced the engine, and I quickly found my way into its driver seat. I was scared, pissed, and crying the whole way home. *How could you Cavalli? How could you?*

By the time Cavalli made it home I'd practically cried all the tears I could cry. But just hearing him enter the house brought more tears. I was sitting at the corner of our bed with a empty wine glass dangling from my hand when he entered. He instantly began disrobing, preparing for our would-be dinner date.

From the angle in which I sat, Cavalli couldn't see my face. "Jordyn," he said with a toss of his dirty clothes towards the hamper. "Why ain't you dressed? Didn't you get the text? I told you—" but when he rounded the corner and noticed the wine glass in my hand, he stopped in his tracks. "What's wrong, Baby? Everything a'ight?" His words brought even more tears to my eyes. He asked again.

I lifted my head and pierced him with my green, dagger-tipped eyes. "I saw it," I said coldly. "I saw it Cavalli. All of it."

"You saw what? What did you see?" he questioned, trying to play me for Boo-Boo the fool.

"That *fucking shit* in the trunk!" I yelled. I know I sounded corny cursing, being that I rarely did it, but I was pissed off. Really pissed off!

"You had no business goin' in there, Jordyn," he said in a tone that suggested I was wrong and not him.

"What? I had no business?" I huffed. "I had no business? So you knew?"

Cavalli sighed and shook his head. "Why did you look, Jordyn? You were just supposed to go from point A and point B. You had no business—"

I threw the wine glass against the wall near his head. "I caught a fucking flat, Cavalli! A flat!" I yelled. Cavalli didn't speak, just looked. "How could you? How could you? I thought you loved me, Cavalli? I thought you loved me," I sobbed.

Cavalli moved closer, cautiously. "I do love you, Jordyn," he said softly. "You know I do."

I took two steps back. "You couldn't possibly love me, Cavalli. If you did, you would've told me you dealt drugs. And you sure as hell wouldn't have set me up like that. You don't do that to people you love."

"But—but it's not like that, Jordyn."

"It's not like what? What, you don't deal drugs, or you didn't put me in harm's way? Which one is it Cavalli? Which one?"

"I didn't—"

I slammed my fist against the vanity attached to our dresser. "Stop it! Just stop fucking lying to me Cavalli! Just stop!" Glass shattered and showered the beige-carpeted-flooring creating thousands of tiny reflections of my pain-filled face.

Cavalli looked as if he were about to lie, but for the anger etched in my face he opted against it. "I was wrong," he admitted. "I was absolutely wrong, Jordyn. I lied and I'mma piece of shit it for it. I never meant to hurt you. I thought I was slick. I thought I could hide it in the trunk and you'd never know." For some reason Cavalli's honesty lightened my heart a little bit. "And whether you believe it or not, I knew where you were the whole time. I knew you were safe. Nothing could've gone wrong Jordyn. Nothing."

I shot Cavalli this crazy look. My face was contorted and my eyes piercing.

"Just hear me out," he said with his hands out before his chest. "…I had eyes on you the entire time. The entire time, Jordyn. Ever since you left the house earlier you were being followed." I wanted to speak—to cuss his black ass out—but the words wouldn't produce. "You were the only one I could trust, Jordyn. I had nobody else. One of my workers been clippin' my stash, and—"

"Who are you? Runners? Clipping your stash? Who… what, are you?"

Cavalli took me by the hand. "I'm the man you fell in love with, Jordyn. I'm your man."

I pulled away. "Bullshit. Bullshit, Cavalli. And you know it. You know I never would've dealt with you had I known you were dealin' dope. You're not the man I love. You're an imposter."

Cavalli grabbed my hand again. "And again," he said with soft eyes. "You're right. You're absolutely right, Jordyn. I did know that. And that's exactly why I didn't tell you."

"So you lied to me?"

"But I didn't lie," he maneuvered.

I scowled.

"But I didn't," he said.

"You didn't? So what do you call it? What, withholding the truth?"

"Withholding the truth is more like it. I didn't lie to you though Jordyn. I've never lied to you. When we first met I told you I was an investor, and I am. You knew about the cars, the houses, the jewelry, and the clubs and restaurants—"

"But not about the drugs?" I cut in. "You just conveniently forgot to add the fact that you're a drug smuggler."

Cavalli chuckled

"Oh, and it's funny?" I questioned with my fist balled up tight.

"No, no," he said smiling with his hands out front his face. "It's just, you're so cute when you're mad."

I stopped and waved my finger back and forth in his face. "No. Hu-unn. Don't even try it." Cavalli definitely wasn't about to charm his way out of this one.

"What? I'm serious," he said and walked up and put his hands on my shoulders. "You're beautiful when you're mad. I love the way your nose scrunches up and your forehead wrinkles like a little pug." He ran his finger over my lumpy forehead. "See, you look like a little feisty puppy. Gimme a hug... Gimme a hug, girl."

Cavalli put his arms around me and hugged me tight. He put his chin on the top of my head and sighed. "I'm so sorry, Jordyn. I really am. I love you, and I need you to know that. Everything I do, I do it for us. I just wanna see you happy, baby. I ain't never been crazy for a woman the way I am about you. I trust you. I trust you with my life, Jordyn. The way you trust me with yours, right?" Cavalli paused, leaned back and looked at me. "Wait... You do trust me, don't you?" I shook my head, slightly. "Just not with your life, huh? Oh, I see. I trust you with my entire life and you only trust me a little, huh? I see how it is... Guess we were both hidin' something then."

Cavalli removed his arms and turned his back on me, walked to the end of the bed. He dropped his head and took a deep breath.

Cavalli looked as if he were about to cry. It made me give it some thought. I did trust Cavalli. And I trusted him with my life. But he hurt me. Before that, no one had ever hurt me like that. I mean, I loved that man's dirty drawers. I'm serious. No one could've told me that Cavalli was even near capable of doing something wrong in the magnitude of what he's just done. I would've practically bet my life that he was a legitimate businessman. Drugs? Guns? No. Not my man. I would've never—ever!—thought that he'd be wrapped up in anything like that. So yes, I was hurt. But in a way, I understood Cavalli's plight. I was his other half, his better half, and he should've been able to trust me, trust me with his life. I just wished he would've kept me out of his nefarious dealings. I mean, what was next? Me preparing and dealing drugs on the street corners with him? Most certainly not. But, I had to let him know how I felt. I had to. I at least owed him that.

"Cavalli," I said to the top of his head, "I do trust you. I trust you with my life. I just... I just... I never expected anything like that." By now Cavalli was looking me square in the eye, his eyes weary and near moist. "You worried me, baby. I was scared. Real scared."

Cavalli stood to his feet. "Worried? Worried about what? I told you, Jordyn, I'd never let anything happen to you. Never."

"And I'm not even supposed to fraction in the worst case scenario?"

"Yes. I mean, no. It's just... Jordyn, you have to trust me. I know what I'm doin'."

"That *sounds* good, Cavalli. It really does. But what if something was to happen? What if the cops catch me? Then what?" By now my eyes were tearing back up and my cheeks were shiny with tears.

Cavalli stood and wiped a tear from my cheek. "Nothing like that is ever gonna happen, Jordyn. Not to you, not to me. I promise. I gotta couple more moves to make, and I'm out. I'm done. For good."

"Then what?" I asked. "Then what's supposed to happen? Me and you in paradise or something?"

"You're absolutely right."

"That easy?"

"That easy," he repeated.

Although I wanted more, more confirmation, I could see the sincerity in his eyes. "And you promise you'll never keep anything from me ever again?" I asked. "Nothing?"

Cavalli gazed into my eyes with a look of intent so deep that I would've believed him had he said that grass was blue and the sky green. "My word, Jordyn. I love you, and I never want to see you hurtin' again."

I leaned up on my tippy-toes and kissed Cavalli on the lips. "I believe you, Cavalli. I do. I don't know how, but I do. I just need to know one more thing. Well, two... First, I need to know if you were behind those extra sixteen boxes on our purchase order, and if so, what was it in those boxes. And, secondly, I really need to know exactly what does a couple more moves consist of. Because I can't do this Cavalli."

Cavalli took a deep breath. "Well, first off..." he said giving me direct eye contact. "Yes, I was behind those extra boxes. It was heroin. Afghanistan's our leading supplier nowadays, and it's cheaper if I find my own transportation."

"How long has this been happening?"

"I been getting my product from there for the last few years, but a light bulb went off when you decided we should import our own goods from there."

"Did you ever put the orders in my name?"

"Never. Always in Jessica's name."

"Is she really an accountant?"

"Yes. And a good one. And before you even ask, no, I never dealt with her on an intimate or emotional level."

"Good for clearing that up for me. And as for my second question?"

"Well," he said looking to the ceiling, assumingly searching for a better way to convey his message, "The best way to put this, is… Well, what you saw today, that was only a quarter of what's left. There's three quarters left."

"Fuck, Cavalli! That entire god-damned trunk was filled with shit. What type of dealer are you?"

Cavalli laughed. "A big one," he said somewhat modestly. "But, it won't take much longer. Maybe three, four months tops."

"And then it's over?" I asked, more like I wished, with my mouth and my heart.

"Then it's over. I promise," he said

"I love you, Cavalli. Always and forever."

Cavalli kissed me softly on the lips. "Always and forever," he said back. "Forever and always, I'll love you too…"

<u>Chapter Ten</u>

Nearly three months had passed since my very unwanted and unwarranted discovery of Cavalli's illicit lifestyle, and while I didn't approve of it, I came to understand it more. And for some reason, I wanted to. Probably because I was a supportive person by nature, or probably because I was just intrigued by the lifestyle. I don't know. What I do know, though, is that there's drugs everywhere nowdays, and after so long that stuff just grows on you. Before long you start wanting to know where the stuff comes from, the effects it has on its users, and if you're like me—very inquisitive—you wanted to know the prices and measurements on everything.

I asked Cavalli question after question until he finally just caved. "You know what?" he said. "I'mma let you see for yourself." The next thing I knew, I was being thrust head first into the under world; packaging, distribution, I saw it all. I even saw a guy come close to OD'ing. His name was Frank, and he usually tested all of Cavalli's product before it hit the streets. He was tall, very thin, and had strong pungent odor emanating from him. Frank was the first true junkie I'd ever met. He carried a small pouch in his front pant pocket that held his "tools".

Frank was extremely comfortable around me. He sat down, took out his syringe, spoon, and lighter, and within six minutes he was "tied off" and a big brown vein bulging from his right arm. Frank punctured the skin (with the tip of what I'm sure was a dirty needle) and struck blood. He pulled back on the plunger a tad, causing blood to mix with the dark-brown toxic sludge inside the barrel of the syringe, and teased it until he had a good blend. Frank eased the mixture into his vein and patiently waited on the dose to take effect. He leaned back in the dirty green recliner chair, and closed his eyes and five minutes later was convulsing.

Cavalli quickly grabbed a small zip-lock bag of ice from Frank's freezer—which seemed to be awaiting this very day—and poured it down the front of Frank's pants. The reaction was a bit offset, but the bits of frozen water served their purpose. Frank gasped, grabbed at his crotch, and sat up wide eyed. A string of slobber hung from his bottom lip like a venomous spider from a thick web. He'd just come back from the dead. "Oh... Oh yeah... That's it. That's— that's it right there, baby boy... Good mix. Damn good mix."

That was Frank. High as the heavens above, more moved by the mixture of the dope than the fact that he'd almost lost his life testing it. Crazy huh? I'd never seen anything like it. Who congratulates the person who almost kills them? This was the craziest thing I'd ever seen.

So, yeah, Cavalli exposed me to a lot more of the street life once he saw that I wasn't as repulsed by it the way I was in the beginning. It was entertaining. Like when I was in middle school and I learned about the lost Pygmy tribe of Africa, or the Barbaric Celtic Warriors of Ireland. The streets were incredibly interesting. There was so many things I didn't know. For instance, I never knew cocaine came from Columbia, and that the locals produced it and distributed it abroad for proceeds that ranged from the millions—sometimes billions—of dollars annually. Nor did I know that the majority of the heroin saturating the streets of the U.S. came from Afghanistan and China, and that it was generally smuggled through foreigners with temporary media visas (or, in rare cases, through an approved vendor, such as World Inc., the company Cavalli and I used to import goods for Jordyn's.)

I learned so much about the streets, in so little time, and I was proud of Cavalli for being honest with me. He was so much more comfortable now that I knew. No more double lifestyles or secret societies. For him, I was in it till the end. Well, not actually. Okay, sort of. Well, we'll just say I was more comfortable knowing things than not knowing. I liked seeing my man happy. I liked watching him do his thing, loved seeing him order people around and orchestrate things the way he did. Cavalli was a businessman. Probably just as good in the underworld as he was in the normal world. Maybe even better now that he didn't have to tip-toe around. He could conduct his multi-million dollar deals like the true boss he was, and if he needed help from his Queen, he could get it. I knew how to operate the money counters and shrink-wrap cash now, and although I didn't particularly like being around when he did it, I knew how to re-package the kilos after Cavalli "cut" them. I know a lot of you say I was silly or stupid for dealing with that type of stuff—especially coming from my squeaky-clean background—but I loved Cavalli, and if he couldn't trust me, then who else could he trust?

*   *   *

Five minutes after four o'clock Cavalli exited the back door of Jordyn's in route to meet his supplier. "Be back 'round six," he said with a brown box filled with shrink-wrapped cash in hand. "Make sure you're lookin' out for Che and Cody... They should be here in the next hour to snatch up the situation for Boston. 'Member what I told you to tell 'em right?"

"Of course. You told me to tell them to use the back door this time, and that they're gonna have to box it up on their own. Is that right?"

Cavalli smiled his beautiful smile. "That's right. Thank you, babe."

I smiled back. "You know I got you, daddy. What time you comin' back?"

"Umm, Probably around eight or nine. They got me meetin' 'em in Columbus this time. I'm thinkin' two hours there, one hour back. Don't worry though. I'll be home as soon as possible." Cavalli blew a kiss at me, I caught it, pressed it against my lips, and watched him walk out the service entry with enough money in his arms to feed a small country.

The next few minutes would change my life forever...

I was busy taking inventory when I heard the back door swing open. At first I thought it was Cavalli, that maybe he had left something behind and was coming back to fetch it real quick so he could be back on his merry way. But when I heard their voices, and saw the three masked figures through the narrow entranceway, I knew that wasn't the case.

"Don't move!" one of the men yelled and pointed his pistol at my head.

"The—the money's in the register," I stammered. "Just take it. Take it and leave."

"Don't fuck wit' me, bitch!" he shouted and shoved the barrel of the gun further in my face. "Where it at?!"

"I don't—"

"I said don't fuck wit me! The money and the dope, where it at?!"

I paused. "I don't, I don't know about any money or dope. All I have is—is—what's in the register. Please take it and leave."

"Bitch! We know it's here. Now where it at!"

My first thought was the Boston Package. Fifty kilo's of cocaine and twenty kilos of heroin. But I was sure that they'd kill me or harm me if I turned it over. So I did what I thought was the smartest thing to do. I lied. "I don't—I don't know who told you there was something in here, but they lied. We don't carry much money, and I swear to God I don't know about any—" I didn't manage another word before the taller gunman swung his pistol and violently hit me upside the head with it. The hard steel crashed against my temple and brought me to my knees instantly. My brain shook, eyes watered, and my knees felt like rubber balls.

"Next time it's gonna be a bullet!" he yelled believingly. "Now, where the fuck the shit at?!"

I wanted to speak—to boldly tell another lie—but I couldn't. I couldn't move my lips. The blunt blow rattled my entire insides and the warmth from the blood gushing out my head further solidified my silence. I was scared senseless. But my silence wasn't stopping them. They were determined, and on a serious mission. They were out to get paid. "You, check upstairs," the taller one said to the more stumpier of the three. "And you," he pointed to the skinniest, "You check the back closet... Sometimes it's in boxes marked 'imports'."

Upon his orders, both took off immediately in their assigned directions. I instantly felt a surge of panic and anger overcome me. The blatant act of betrayal was sickening and transparently obvious. It had to be either Che or Cody behind the robbery. No one else. They were the only two privy to that type of information. But neither of the three were Che or Cody. Or were they? I gave the masked figure before me a quick once-over. Nope. And I was sure neither of the others weren't Che or Cody either. Too skinny, too stumpy. I'd spent too much time around those two to know it wasn't them. I was a hundred percent sure. But they had to be involved. We were the only four people who knew about the Boston Package. Surely Cavalli wouldn't stage an act of betrayal against himself, and I damned sure wasn't that heartless and brazen. It was no other choice. It was Che and Cody behind it.

After a short time both men rushed back into the room. "Nothing," they seemed to say at the same time. "Nothin' at all."

"Nothing?" The ringleader asked. "No cash or D? You check the boxes good?"

"No boxes marked imports, no cash."

"Me either," said Stumpy. "Nuthin'."

Even through his mask, I could tell the ringleader was enraged. His eyes were red and the fabric above his nose was scrunched up in a knot. "That shit gotta be in here somewhere. It gotta be!"

"I mean, it was boxes," said Skinny, "But nothin' in 'em. Nothin' but nuts and cakes and shit. Want me to check again?"

"Check again. We ain't leavin' here empty-handed," said the leader.

"Got it," said Skinny said and tapped Stumpy. "Come on!" They both took off in their assigned directions. And just like before, they returned with nothing.

"Nothing."

"Nothing, man."

The leader pointed his gun at my temple. "You know we ain't leavin' here empty-handed, right?"

"But—but I don't know what you're talking about. The money's in the regist—"

Before I could get out another word, he hit me again. This time much harder. I winced and held my hand where the blood was pouring out. "Bitch! I swear to God you better hope that nigga give a fuck about you!" He looked over at Stumpy. "Blindfold that bitch," he said. "And get her hands, too. She comin' wit' us... Either that nigga gon' pay, or we gone torture this bitch... C'mon, let's get the fuck outta here!"

After covering my eyes with a black bandana, and my hands with plastic zip-ties, I was yanked to my feet and dragged outside. They threw me into a trunk, slammed it shut, and jerked off doing about 40 or 50 miles per hour. I felt like I could've died in there. Being bound in a trunk is some of the scariest shit ever! The fear of a wreck, being left inside to rot, and being shot while inside this dark, dungeonous cave was terrifying. Even after they opened the trunk and pulled me out, I trembled. All I could do was think of how I should've gave 'em what they came for, that it was right there in their face. All I had to do was hand it to them. Now look at what I'd gotten myself into. I just knew I was about to die.

When I was finally pulled out and on my feet, I heard the taller guy say, "Get that bitch in the house and tie 'er up downstairs! Now!" That's when I got lucky. Due to the blood running down my face so freely, and the way the blindfold was tied so loosely, I was able to wiggle my forehead and make the bandana slide down a tad bit. Now I could see where I was. I saw a Popeye's Chicken, and the banner for a newly renovated Black African Soul Hair and Beauty Supply Store. I knew exactly where I was. *Big blue house, white trim... Right near the new beauty supply store. Salem Avenue. God I pray they don't kill me.*

They took me down a flight of stairs and into a dim basement. It was damp, grungy, and a boiler or furnace of some sort sat humming in the near distance. They sat me next to an old pipe extending from a cement wall and immediately began their interrogation. "The Boston Package?... Where it at?... And the rest of the dope?... Where the money at?... How much cash and jewelry at the crib?... Why you holdin' out?... You know we gon' get it anyway, right?... Why you holdin' out?!"

I held out for as long as I could. I believed my silence was my only bargaining chip. But, my antics only lasted for about a total of three minutes. The leader cocked his gun, pressed the barrel to my forehead, and said, "Go get the bleach... I'mma 'bout 'ta kill dis bitch!"

I didn't want to die. I was so young. I had so much living to do. I still hadn't been on a cruise boat, and I wasn't married with a big house on the hill and two kids. I couldn't die. "Okay—okay!" I yelled. "I'll tell you. Just don't shoot me," I pled. "I'll tell you. Please!"

"Bitch, you better. 'Cause I'm gettin' real fuckin' impatient wit' yo' ass." I could smell the oil from his weapon. One slight squeeze and I was done. My life over.

"Okay, I'll tell you... I'll tell you. Just don't shoot."

"I'm listenin'," he said and waited. "And bitch, you better make it good. "

"I have about... about seven grand in the bank, and probably another twenty in jewelry if you let me go to get it."

The three broke out in laughter. Not the good type of laughter though. Not the type of heart-healthy laughter brought on by a child or a silly co-worker. It was mockery.

"I can sign over my Mercedes, too. "

They laughed louder. Then the leader spoke: "Man, this bitch don't get it."

"She can't," one of the others responded. "She definitely can't."

"Yeah, I know. But how 'bout you tell 'er, Scrap. "

"No doubt, Big Bruh," I heard him say. Then he walked near me. I could feel the heat from his pant leg was near my face. "Listen, bitch," he said forcefully, "We know everything. We know about the packages, the money, everything. Now, either you tell us what you know, or we gon' torture you 'til you get the message. You ever been fucked wit' a broken bottle to you cum blood? Huh, bitch? How 'bout havin' your fingernails yanked off one by one 'til your whole body goes numb?" I cringed at the thought. "I know," he said. "But it's your call. It's all on you. Either you can tell what we need to know, right here right now, or you can die wishin' you did. It's your call."

I believed them. Every single word. In fact, I believed them so much that I knew I couldn't tell them the truth, that I lied in the beginning about the Boston Package. They'd kill me for sure. *My only option is lie again*, I said to myself. *Lie, Lie,Lie!*

"He took the Boston Package with him," I said. "He said he was going to meet his friends Che and Cody." Hopefully the sound of their partners' name would strengthen my lie. " He told me to tell 'em the plans changed, that he was taking care of it himself, that he had a bad feeling about something—I think cops. He walked out the back door with a brown box in his hands and that's all I know. He don't tell me everything. I only see what he wants me to see. I promise. Now please... Let me go."

Silence. I could tell they were searching one anothers face, asking if they should trust me. Did my naming the other culprits (Che and Cody) lend plausibility to my spiel. I was praying it did.

"Take that bandana off!" the leader said. "Now! Raise her head... Hurry up! We need this nigga to know this ain't no joke. Yeah, let 'em see the blood... That's it." Stumpy put his gun to my head and the other guy took a picture. There was a flash from his camera phone. "Now cover that bitch up. He got twenty-four hours to meet the ransom, or this bitch dead. It went black again and the sound of the creaky wooden stairs filled the basement. I dropped my head and started praying. Only God could help me. Only God could save me. *Lord please let Cavalli comply. Lord please... I'm too young to die.*

<u>Chapter Eleven</u>

I wiggled my nose compulsively until the blindfold slipped down far enough to grant me partial vision. Two of my three captors were standing nearby, but neither were familiar to me. They both wore dark jeans and black long-sleeved shirts, and both of their weapons were visible.

"How much of that dope left?" asked the stumpier of the two, in a tone that insisted he was second in command. The skinny guy—the man upstairs— was most certainly the head hunch of the trio.

The third wheel reached in his pants pocket and removed a small plastic baggie with a tan powdery substance in it. He fumbled it between his fingers loosely and tilted his head sideward a bit. "Bout umm… Bout um… A G or two."

Stumpy clicked his tongue against the roof of his mouth and smiled a mischievous grin. "Yeah," he said with a rub of his crotch through his faded black denim jeans. "We gone need it fo' what we bout 'ta do to dis hoe… Hey! Hey!" he yelled at me. I quickly dropped my head so he couldn't see that I could see. "You ever had some dope dick, pretty lady? Huh? Have you? Answer me, bitch!" he yelled and started my way.

"No-No," I stammered quickly. "Please."

He laughed. "Now which is it? No, or please?" His footsteps didn't progress. He was stationary, rubbing his crotch. "Yeah, well, this shit right here make fo' the best fuckin'… Yup. I get this situation right here in me, and, ooooohhwee!" he sounded off, his voice shrieking and reverberating through the damp muggy basement, sending a chill through me almost as cold as the one I got when they threw me in their trunk. I took a deep breath and lifted my head. They were both standing at a small circular table in the center of the basement. It stood about three feet tall, and was completely littered with magazines, ashtrays, and old beer bottles.

"Dope dick, pretty lady," the other said, "…it's the type a dick a bitch'll neva—"

"Neva!" the other chimed in.

"—Forget!" he continued before violently removing everything from the table—magazines, ashtrays, bottles—dumping the entire contents of the plastic baggie on the bare table. "Dope Dick…" he cheesed, head bent over the table, nostrils inches away from the small pile of powder he'd just laid down. "…Dope Dick da type a dick dat every hoe,"—he took a large whiff— "of every creed and denomination, need." He took another whiff, a stronger whiff, inhaling the majority of the pile in two sniffs.

"Hey, nigga!" his partner yelled at him. "Fuck you doin'?! You cray or some shit. You know T-Bone's shit uncut. What you tryna do, O.D. befo' we fuck dis hoe?" Just as he said that, the blind fold slipped. I wiggled my head to maintain my view. Shit.

"Damn, Nigga," Stumpy said to his partner with a hard rub of his wide nose. "Fuck you didn't tell me that shit from the be-gin? Good thing… Good thing Im'ma vet at dis shit…" His voice had already trailed off as he rocked on the balls of his feet.

"Yeah, well, you better hope so," the other said. "'Cause I ain't callin' no cops or no ambulance. We gone fuck dis hoe, torture dis bitch, and collect dis loot. Ain't got time," he paused as he leaned down and took a light whiff of the product himself—a cautious one though— and followed it with: "Damn! Yeah… Oh, yeah! Oh yeah! Dis hoe gettin' some heavy wood today baby… Betta make sure… Make sure everything in order before Teeze come back. Don't want… Don't want the bossman to find out we slippin' on the job. Ya dig? That shit cost us a lotta bread last time we slipped up. I need… I need all mine, today." He rubbed his face, sniffled, and took off slowly up the old creaky stairs mumbling to himself.

As soon as he was up the stairs, I cut my eye at the other felon. He grabbed at his crotch lustfully and rubbed his nose. "Bout'ta make… bout'ta make dis a night… A night…to… to…" he dragged and rubbed, on his way towards me. "Yeeeeaaah," he said with a tug of his belt. He pulled at his buckle, unclasped it and removed his limp penis. The harsh reality of what was about to take place dug further into my conscience, creating a sickening feeling in my stomach. I was bound, partially blindfolded, and about to be raped. Why was God punishing me like this?

Within seconds he was close enough for me to see that he was uncircumcised and above average. A second later, I could smell—almost taste—the stench of his stinky crotch. It was tangy, acrid. A smell so strong I almost threw up in my mouth. Sickening. Absolutely sickening.

"Oooh, yeah," he said jerking himself drunkenly in front of me. He rested his left hand on my right shoulder, and with the right began to guide himself towards my mouth. "Oh…" he mumbled almost lifelessly, "Oh… Oh… Oh y-yeah…" he said and gasped. Suddenly my captor's body started jerking. But not jerking as though he were jerking-off. Jerking as in convulsing, jerking. He squeezed my shoulder tightly—real tightly—and fell hard against the wall. The smell of his crotch grew stronger, intoxicating, and his penis touched my face. Ugh! I almost died inside. The very spot where his penis landed against my face felt as if it had been burned by some sort of chemical agent, like Agent Orange or Anthrax. I yanked my head away quickly, bumping my head on the corner of the wall almost splitting it. He gripped my shoulder tighter and rocked on his feet. "Urgh… Urghhhh," he hissed and teetered to a fall. His body crashed hard against the cold concrete flooring, pistol sliding to a stop just inches away from my foot. I looked down at the pistol, then back over at my captor. He was convulsing, white foam spitting from the corners of his mouth like the homemade volcanoes you make in school, hands up around his throat, as if trying to physically fight back the powerful drug that was aggressively overloading his system. He made one more wet gurgling sound, then kicked his feet and hissed. Three seconds later, I was springing into action.

I rifled through his pockets roughly in a frantic search for something sharp enough to cut through the plastic zip ties on my wrist. Nothing. Cell phone, car keys, cigarettes, lighter. I had to get free. Then it hit me: The bottles! The beer bottles that'd crashed violently against the ground when the two were preparing themselves to rape me were right there. A shard! Right near his head. I scooted towards it on my knees, hands tied before me, and just as I was about to grab it, I heard the other guy yell out, "Hey! Hey! What the fuck you do to my homeboy?!" from the top of the basement stairs. I looked up and he was lunging down towards me. I reached out and scooped up the gun with my palms. It was heavy and slipped a bit, but my finger found the trigger like a newborn baby to its mother's tit. I pulled back, *Bang*! Then again, and again. *Bang! Bang! Bang!* Smoke leapt from his chest and his expressions changed quickly. He went from angry, to utter-pain, to lifeless. He lost his footing and missed the last two steps, his arms flying about wildly as he crashed chin first against the concrete. First there was a crack—bones breaking— then blood. It sprayed out like a split waterhose, spraying the entire basement floor with cherry-red gooey stuff. There was no doubt he was dead. The other guy too. But I started to send a bullet through both their heads anyway just to be sure. Lord knows what they would've done had fate not been on my side.

I quickly reached out for the first guy's cell phone. Seven-One-Eight-Three-Two-Two-Four... *Answer   Cavalli. Answer. Answer please. Answer Cavalli. Please answ—*

"Hello?" His voice was angelic. "Hello?" I was so happy to hear his voice I froze. "Hello?" he said again.

"Ca-Cavalli?" I sobbed. "They tried to kill me… They tried to kill me."

"Jordyn? Jordyn is that you? Where you at baby? Where? I know exactly where you are. I'm on may way. Keep that gun in your hand and stay alert. I'm not far away."

I couldn't understand why Cavalli wanted me to stay put, opposed to getting the furthest away from there as possible, but the first thing he did when he entered the house was ask me where they were. "We gotta get rid of the bodies," he said. I fell into his arms and pointed towards the basement.

"They're down there," I cried. "They're down there. Both of 'em. They were gonna—they were gonna *kill* me."

"Calm down, Baby. Just calm down. I need you to focus. I need you to stay right here while I—"

"No. No, Baby. Please don't leave me here. No. Please don't ever leave me again." Cavalli placed both of his hands on my face to calm me down, explained how he was just gonna run outside to the car and be right back. He quickly checked the bullets in the gun I took from my captors, placed it back into my hands and pulled his from his waistline. He darted outside, quickly returned with two gas cans in hand, and immediately began covering up for my crimes. First he made me wash my hands with gasoline, a method used apparently by murderers to remove GSR(gunshot residue), and then instructed me to "douse" the lower quarters of the home while he tended to the remainder. Three minutes later we were scurrying out the front door and the house was engulfed in flames. There was no doubt the house was burned to the ground by the time the fire department got there. I was just glad I wasn't in their while it was burning.

*Thank God for blessing me with him... Lord knows I couldn't have made it out of there without my baby. I owe him the world...*Lord thank you for delivering me to him...

$$* \qquad * \qquad *$$

I sat in the steamy hot bath staring blankly at the wall as Cavalli questioned. "What else did they say?" he asked in a soft undertone the belied his patience yet highlighted the wrath boiling within him. Cavalli loved me dearly. He was hurt. Deeply, deeply, hurt.

"They said the name Tez, or Teeze," I replied with my eyes fixated on a small stretch of caulking between the Egyptian tiles in the bathroom. It seemed to be the same color as the narcotics my captors were sniffing.

"You said *Teeze*? You sure? *MOTHERFUCKER!*" he shouted and slammed his hand against the sink. Handsoap and toothbrushes flew across the room, startling me. He grabbed my head and pressed it against his chest. "I'm sorry, Baby. I'm so sorry. About everything. It's Che and Cody. Teeze is their man. Those giddy motherfuckers Stamps and Stix were his hired hands." He patted my head and wiped my wet mane as if I were a distraught child. "Im'ma kill 'em both. Wit' my own hands. I ain't gone pay no fuckin' dopefiends to do the job for me, hidin' in the shadows like a bitch. Nah, Im'ma tune dem muffuckaz up on my own..." Cavalli began rocking and patting me at the same time. I knew he was about to do something crazy. Very crazy. And as bad as I wanted to stop him, I knew there was no use. Cavalli was a man madly in love, and Che and Cody had just tore a hole in his heart. They were about to die a violent death. A very violent death. And they deserved every bit of it. Death before dishonor. Death before dishonor…

<u>Chapter Twelve</u>

Dayton Daily News headlines read: ***SLAIN LOCALS FOUND OUTSIDE OF PROBLEMATIC NIGHT CLUB***.
As the reporter reported, two African-American males were sitting idle inside a silver Mercedes Benz when a black SUV of some sort pulled alongside and the driver of that SUV opened fire. The papers called it an "ambush" and used other modifying terms such as "hit" "overkill" and "gangland style" to describe the level of gruesomeness and brutality of the crime, but I wasn't really moved. The victims were identified as Cody Glenn and Che Tizo (AKA Che and Cody), and that hit came from Cavalli himself. There was no mistaking that. I didn't care how they were killed, so long as they were dead. And the way he spoke of the night of the incident (one that he made me swear to never speak of again) I knew their days were numbered. I knew Cavalli would kill them, and I knew he'd make a statement of it. That's the way the underworld worked. When stuff like that happened, it had to be addressed, quickly. "Dese niggas like wolves out here, Bay," Cavalli explained afterwards. "They get one whiff of blood and they salivatin'..." So I truly understand why he felt compelled to make the statement he did: ***Don't fuck with Cavalli or his family! Don't fuck with his money, and don't fuck with his business, period!.*** And so what if it took forty-two rounds from a military-issue assault rifle to do it. As long as the point was made, all was well. Besides,

when you act like scum, you get taken for scum, period. And nobody wants scum around, right?

Anyhow, my life was a lot better knowing they were gone. I mean, I was still shaky as hell, but knowing they'd never be back to haunt me was a lot more settling than not. I couldn't have them roaming around freely. It would've drove me crazy, looking over my shoulder every five seconds. They had to die. And I know it sounded crazy but they had to go.

Nothing had surfaced about the Teeze guy, and that still worried me, but if I knew anything about Cavalli, he'd get him soon or later. He'd definitely get him soon or later…

I stayed with Tish and Remy for the first couple weeks after the incident, but it wasn't all that fulfilling. Keeping the truth from my own family was killing me from the inside out. I felt like and international spy, someone who'd infiltrated enemy soil. I wanted to talk about it, especially to Tish, my BFF, but I'd never be able to deal with Cavalli afterwards if I did. Me, Jordyn, with a drug dealer? Hell no. Especially one of his magnitude. And I couldn't even begin to fathom how she'd react when I told her that I was kidnapped and had to kill one of my captors in order to escape. I'd never see Cavalli again. Ever! So I lied. "Nothing's wrong, Tish," I mislead, while out on a girl's night out. "Cavalli and I are great," I said. "Absolutely great." There's no way she could've seen through that. My facial expressions belied the truth, and my tone wasn't offset or pitchy. She'd never find out. Never.

Tish stirred her martini, bit the green olive dangling from her straw in half, and turned her lips up. "And I suppose you left your mansion out there in the 'burbs just for the hell of it, huh? Girl you must be silly. I know you, Jordyn. Probably better than you know yourself. Now quit BS'ing and tell me what's goin' on. He on crack or somethin'?"

I spit out a mouthful of my tie-dye Mytie drink. "What?! No. Crack? Why would you assume he was a crackhead?" I asked laughing. "Hell no. Never."

"Then what is it?" she asked. "He beatin' you? I'm tellin' you, if he put his hands on you, I'll kill 'em! You know I just got my gun license girl," she said and drew a small automatic handgun from her purse. "Learned how to shoot it too." Tish held the gun to her side like an old cowboy and mouthed, *Bang, Bang, Bang.*

"Girl! If you don't put that away. And where did you get that from anyway? Remy know about it? 'Cause you know if he find out he'll kill you."

"No he won't girl," she said confidently as she put the gun back in her purse. "He's the one who bought it. Remember I told you about my stalker?" Now, she didn't really have a stalker. More like someone who happened to "coincidentally" be in the wrong place at the wrong time, one too many times.

"Who, the creepy mailman?" I asked.

"Yup. The creepy mailman," she admitted agreeingly. "I told Remy, and, well, *she,*" she said emphasized her point by patting her Gucci purse, "was the conclusion of that convo. I finished my CCW class three weeks ago, and I

97

already have six hours of," —She fixed her thumb, index and middle finger to resemble a gun— "shooting hours." She drew back her imaginary weapon and blew smoke from its barrel. "I can give you my instructor's number if you want," she said happily, which was actually a good idea. I know it'd make me feel a lot safer, and it'd definitely cut out a lot of avoidable troubles in the event I ever had to use a gun again. I couldn't imagine ever doing time. What would I wear, what would I eat, and where would I sleep? OMG. Who'd do my hair and nails? Who'd arch my eyebrows? Would the food even be edible? And what about sex? Who'd please Cavalli? Would he leave me if I got arrested? Lord God I couldn't get arrested.

"Yeah, give me his number," I said.

"Okay, its—wait. So he *did* put his hands on you?" she asked, her eyes aimed at me as if they were daggers of her own. *Oh my God. I hadn't thought of that. This woman doesn't miss a beat!*

"No, Tish," I pressed out. "No. He didn't put his hands on me."

"You promise? You wouldn't lie to me right would you?" Her eyes were flaming balls of fire, investigating every line and pore on my face. I couldn't lie to that woman if I tried with all my might.

"No. I'm not lying, Tish. I promise. Cavalli never put his hands on me."

"Never?" she asked again, searchingly.

"Never. And he never will. He's not that type of guy. We're good. I just need a little love. It gets lonely out there all by myself, just me and the furniture. And Cavalli won't be back for another two weeks."

"And he's where again?" *I never said where he was, woman.*

"He's away on business." *Ha! Short and sweet.*

"Oh," she said casually, with a cute twirl and sip of her drink. *Here it comes...*

"And he does what again? I mean, aside from buying you hundred-thousand dollar business establishments and whatnot?" *Oh no. We're not doing this.*

I sipped my drink, let the warm sensations from the Ciroc fade a little before I responded. "I told you," I responded in my most chipper tone of voice, "He is an investor."

"Of?" she questioned facetiously, her words hanging in the air like smoke from a pit-fire.

"Of—of a lot of things." *That sounded defensive. That's the last thing I wanna do, sound defensive. She'll pounce all over me. Gotta break away. Break away now!*

I sipped my drink again. Not for the warmth and tingling sensation, but to deflect eye contact and gain strength. I sipped, slowly. Very slowly. "He, um... He invests in all types of things. And business varies depending on the season. He's been in Indiana and Kentucky a lot lately. But we talk and Skype all the time. I just miss him." She was searching. *Sheeze! Stop it! I can't hide anything from this woman!*

"As long as you're happy, Jordyn, that's all that matters." *Now she was serious. She was letting up.* "Nobody deserves to be anything but happy in a relationship," she said. "Make sure you always remember that, okay? We can be miserable on our own. We entertain the thought of companionship with peace, prosperity, and happiness at mind. If you're not achieving it in all ways possible you may as well be by yourself."

She was absolutely correct. And I was happy with Cavalli. We had our couple glitches, but it was almost over. He was almost done. Two or three more months and we were off. Me, Cavalli, Bully the Caine Corso, and the beautiful country life. At least so I thought.

Everything that glitters ain't always gold...

But you can bet for sure that the concrete can bear a rose...

We are in life what we put in.

We are Gods and Goddesses from the beginning to the end...

Chapter 12

Cavalli had been back from his Indiana trip for two whole days and still hadn't touched me. It's like he wasn't happy to see me. I mean, he kissed me when he first walked through the door and told me he missed and loved me, but other than that there were no signs of affection. He didn't brush up against me while I was making pancakes like he used to, nor did he grab me by the waist from behind and whisper sweet things into my ear. He was very displaceant and it was starting to bother me. I didn't understand what was going on. Being displaceant around *me* was the *last* thing he should've been. Especially after all I'd been through. Kidnapped? Attempted rape and murder? All that and you mean to tell me the first thing you do when you come home is ask to help thumb through some cruddy-ass drug money? Hell, he didn't even have the decency to bring in the money counters. Boy oh boy was being a drug dealer's girlfriend a draining job.

It took four days before Cavalli finally touched me. And the sex wasn't all that exhilarating. I missed the old Cavalli. The old-old Cavalli. The one who'd lick my neck and slap my ass as he fucked me from behind… The one who'd reach up and rub my clit while I rode him reverse cowgirl. That was the Cavalli I missed. *My Cavalli.* Where did he go? Did the incident with Che and Cody rob him of his peace and sanity? Or was he still mentally and emotionally in "hustler mode"? I once heard that street hustlers suffer from some of the same symptoms as war vets. And it's not that hard to believe. I mean, bullets pinging off of abandoned buildings in Dayton, Detroit, or Atlanta, are the same as bullets pinging off buildings in Iran and Iraq. The streets were guys like Cavalli's warzone, and the stresses they adhere are nearly identical. They're constantly checking over their shoulder for foreign soldiers (i.e. the local cops) and opposing dignitaries (prosecutors, district attorneys, and Supreme Court justices), and death is always looming. It had to be stressing—I know it was. And it was starting to rub off on me. I was only the fiancée of a hustler—and should've been his wife by now damnit!—and I was already starting to regret my decision of being with him. Would I be able to deal with this? Would I up and leave him how Malik and Jaden had left me in the past? This outcome is something I always feared. I couldn't bear with being second. Not to the streets, not to any gangs or drugs, and damn sure not to another woman. Cavalli was gonna have to make a decision, and he was gonna have to make it soon…

So, anyhow, after our rather passionless round of sex, I phoned Tish and asked if she wanted to catch a bite to eat. Of course she would. She said give her about forty minutes and she'd meet me there. Will do.

Our favorite place to eat was a cozy little bistro within Alexander's Strip mall just off of Interstate Forty-Seven. They served amazing sandwiches and dip, and with all the clothing and dessert shops scattered throughout it was a always perfect little retreat. We'd eat our dogwoods and salami specials, and then skip down to Cinnabon or Jenny

Jays Yogurt Café and make the day complete. It was shop, eat, and relaxation all rolled in one.

*   *   *

Cavalli was dressed and out the door five minutes after we'd had sex. He didn't say much, just that he had a few runs to make and that he'd be home soon after. I nodded, didn't say anything back. To be honest, I didn't really care. Especially if he was still displaced. I hated how awkward it made us, how sullen the house and our relationship was. I needed whatever he was going through to hurry up and be over. Four days was too long. I missed my man!

It was bright and sunny outside of All Eats Bistro. The fall sun was forgiving and the last few honey bees were out buzzing about. Tish and I took the same seats outside underneath the yawning as we always did, sipping our sugary sweet lemonade and watching fellow patrons move about from shop to shop, tasting food and trying on hats and sunglasses, plucking every morsel of life out of the year as possible.

I dipped my sandwich in a cup of tangy Algier sauce, took a small bite and let my eyes roam from the minty green vines and purple tulips that stylishly traced the façade of the Bistro and inhaled. The scene was relaxing and tranquil, and helped me understand a lot more about Cavalli and his contrast in character. Cavalli was the rarity in my life and a commonality amongst the streets. But I loved the way he didn't get caught up in the B.S. most hustlers did. He didn't

103

abuse drugs and he damn sure wasn't the blowing money type. He maintained focus on the business aspect of hustling and tended to his beautiful fiancée and home and I trusted and loved him for that. He was my man and he loved me. Yeah. And so what if he was a little displaced at the moment. All he needed was a good home cooked meal and some solid conversation, that's all. He needed to smile, laugh, and to know that I had his back. The streets would always be second in our life and to my love, and I was gonna express this truth to him as soon as I got home…

I had just finished off the other half of my ruben when Tish caught my attention. "Geeze," she said standing to her feet grabbing her purse. "This lemonade always runs through me. Be right back…" Tish wiped the corners of her mouth with a checkered napkin and shook her head, "Five minutes Jay-Jay. Five minutes."

I kinda zoned out when Tish left. Something about the sun and the humdrum of pedestrians milling about put me in a soft trance. I don't know how long I was gone, but when I focused my eyes there was the blur of a familiar face. I shook my head. Another shake. Was that Cavalli? Couldn't be. Not with his arm locked around the waste of another woman. She was a petite dark-skinned woman with oversized Dior frames and Red Bottoms heels. Her hair was styled in the Big Chop and and she seemed happy with him. *This couldn't be. Not Cavalli. Not my Cavalli. He wouldn't be all giddy with another woman and stern with me. This can't be him, it can't…*

I immediately rose to my feet and started across the narrow street separating the two sides of the businesses. My heart was pounding, stomach turning backflips. I'd die inside if it was him. Completely lose all faith in love. There'd be no way for me to love him if he—

"No," I said aloud as I watched him sit down across from her at a pizza parlor directly across from All Eats. She was beautiful, very beautiful with thick lips, deep dimples and a piercing above her right eye. She had doe-like eyes and long lashes. Foreign. Exotic. Edgy. While I was normal, commonplace, basic. I wanted to cry. I could see why he cheated. I had become mundane, typical. *Why wouldn't he upgrade?* My heart melted when he touched her cheek. Tears poured forth as I stood there destroyed. Cavalli had broke my spirit, completely shattered any faith I had left in a life of love. All I could think of was Jaden and Malik and how it was happening again. I knew it. I knew history would repeat itself. I freaking knew it. But it was what it was. At the end of the day if he wanted her and he could have her. I wasn't gonna tear myself down any more than he already had. I cleaned myself up before Tish came out and made up an excuse to get away. By the time Cavalli came home I'd be long gone. Long freakin' gone…

<u>Chapter 13</u>

I was devastated by Cavalli's disheartening act of disloyalty, but in the end, life had to go on. I had cried all I could cry, questioned myself and God all I could question, and hid out for way too long. I couldn't take it anymore. So I handed the teller at the Country Suites my key card and jumped in my car (the one I bought just before Cavalli and I met), headed back to Tish's and Remy's.

For three whole weeks I pondered my decisions, what I'd do now that Cavalli and I weren't together anymore, and ultimately how I'd avoid him. I didn't wanna see that man, at all. And I do mean at all! Didn't wanna hear his voice or his pathetic pleas or fake apologies. I was done. Completely over Cavalli. Hence, my three week hiatus. I wanted/needed to cut off all ties of communication with him, and I knew that was the only way to do it. So I abandoned my phone, disabled my Instagram, Facebook and Twitter accounts, and left every car, piece of jewelry, and article of clothing he ever bought me right there. I didn't offer any reasoning or nasty expletives scribbled with lipstick on mirrors or paper. I was gone, without a trace, and no one knew where. Of course Tish and Remy knew I was okay, but I wouldn't disclose my location. All they'd do was try to come and offer sympathetic consultations and I didn't want them. All I wanted was a little time to heal. I didn't want foam-covered mocha lattes or homemade peanut butter cookies and dry comedy. I just wanted a little time by myself to sort out the details of my life, that's all. And that's exactly how it went. Three weeks of take out and reservations for one; three weeks of *why, why, why,* and, *no, no, no*, and I was back to my old perky self. Back in my old room at Tish's and Remy's (that was only until I found time to get my own place again), back in my old car, and back bartending at Aphrodisiac's. And I have to say that neither Tish nor Remy could be happier. I mean, after all, I was back home and back bringing more customers in at the club. Couldn't get any better. Hmp. All I needed now was a good 'ol piece of revenge sex...

*   *   *

His name was Derek, and he was absolutely striking. Average height, lean, light-brown skin, with white teeth and a earring in his left ear. He dressed casually (polos and Dockers), and I knew *for sure* he wasn't a street guy. His walk, his talk, his entire disposition told me so. And I know what you're thinking. But I could tell now. After being around Cavalli and his friends and business associates so long, I could differentiate. Derek was a man, a gentleman, and I knew he'd be a perfect candidate for revenge sex. But revenge sex, I still couldn't bring myself to ask about. Yeah, it was true enough that Cavalli had brought a side out of me that I didn't know existed, but I was still Jordyn; I still respected myself as a queen, and my body was still a temple.

So, yeah, I'd been hiding out in hiatus for five days. I was back at the club bartending for four, and already on my third date with Derek. In fact, it was about 10pm and my evening shift had just ended. Derek was offering me a glass of champagne at a padded booth in Aphrodisiacs—I suppose to mellow me out before we headed out for a night of fun and relaxation.—but I was a little offset. I didn't need stimulants or drugs to help me get to where I planned to get in the sack with Derek. All he had to do was take my hand and lead me out of there.

I didn't quite know what Derek had planned, but, I felt I could trust him. Well, for the most part. He had his drink, I said goodbye to Remy and his new bartender, Malika, and were about to be on our way from our booth. That's when I saw Cavalli. *Cavalli?* He broke through the doorway with two of his "friends" (hired security hands) and sped straight over to the table with a scowl on his face I couldn't begin to put into words. His fists were clenched, and both of his goons were clutching their waistlines.

He was pissed!

Oh shit, I thought. That's right. I said it. The first thing that came to my mind was, *Oh shit*. Not, *how did he know where I was*, or, *fuck that cheating bastard*, but *oh shit!*. And I'd seen that look on his face before; right before he killed Che and Cody. Now I was worried. Very worried. And not just for myself. But for Derek as well.

"Jordyn, what you doin', and where the hell you been?" he asked from the edge of the table. He seemed more concerned with the presence of my new companion rather than with the fact that I'd been M.I.A. for three whole weeks.

"I-I-" I stammered before regaining the courage to say: "What do you want Cavalli?"

"What do I want?" he grimaced. "What do I—And who the fuck is this?" he said and flipped the collar on Derek's polo button up shirt.

Derek immediately jumped to his feet. "Don't touch me dude!" he said face to face with Cavalli. "Don't ever touch me!"

Cavalli took his open palms and forced Derek back in his seat. But Derek was standing his ground. He bounced right back up with his fists balled as if he were about to punch Cavalli in the face.

"No, don't—" I yelled. But before I could even finish the sentence one of Cavalli's goons snatched Derek up off his feet.

"Lemme go! Lemme—Urghh!" Derek yelled as his feet bounced off the dark carpeted floor as they dragged him to the front door.

"Leave him alone Cavalli! Leave him alone! That man ain't did nothin' to you!"

Just then, Remy walked up. "What's going on, Jordyn ?" he asked searching my face for an answer. But Cavalli's face said it all. "There a problem Cavalli? Is it?"

"Cavalli's men drug Derek outta here," I sounded off, as if I were tattle-telling on him.

"Your friend, huh?" Cavalli scoffed with a smirk on his face. "He's cool, Rem'. He was a lil' irate so we removed him from the premises, that's all."

Remy didn't take kindly to that. "Removed him from the premises?" he said. "And who the hell do you think you are?" but Cavalli didn't respond quickly enough so Remy continued. "Nah, it don't work like that, chief. My name on this here deed, you understand? Which means I'm the only person removin' people from the premises around here. Is that clear?"

I paused, waiting for the moment. The moment where fireworks exploded, and the two clashed; an explosion that had been brewing for quite some time now, but never happened on the account that they both loved me dearly. But, it never happened. Cavalli's scowl lightened, his facial expressions changed, and he looked at me. "Jordyn," he said softly, "I didn't come all the way down here to cause trouble. I just wanna speak with you, in private. I miss you baby, and I jus' wanna know what's going on. Can you give me that?"

Cavalli watched me intently for a couple seconds, then Remy. He was questioning with his eyes, is what he was doing. But Remy was still on fire. He'd still respect my decision if I wanted to talk to him though. I mean, I was just engaged to this man, and I didn't discuss much of our falling out details with him or Tish, so they didn't know the extent of our disagreement (if that's what you wanted to call it). And besides, Cavalli really loved me and I knew he wouldn't take no for an answer.

"Five minutes," I said. "Five minutes. And I have to be sure that my friend is okay first. He didn't deserve that Cavalli. He didn't. He's a good man."

Cavalli's eye twitched for a quick second, but he accepted the terms of my proposal.

"That's cool. We can check on your friend, then talk in the car, a'ight?"

Remy searched my face again. "It's okay, cousin. I'll be back in five minutes. And I'm right outside. You can watch me from the security camera."

"Cool. But I'm telling you right now, Cavalli, if you try anything, I'ma—"

Cavalli laid his hand on Remy's shoulder. "Don't worry," he said smiling coyly. "You got my word, *Chief.*" Cavalli stuck his hand out for mine but I shoved it away and rose from the table. I didn't want him touching me. Not with the same hands he'd touched her with. There's no telling the way he caressed her, the ways he catered to her and loved her. I was disgusted with him. He repulsed me!

When I made it outside, surprisingly, Derek and Cavalli's goons were standing near Derek's sport's car talking. Derek had a cigarette hanging from his lips (didn't know he smoked) and they seemed to be coaxing him in his anger. He was still pissed off I could tell, and probably embarrassed to pieces for having been roughed up in front of me. But, if Derek only knew Cavalli's power and potential, he'd be grateful. It could've been a lot worse than getting escorted from a table in Aphrodisiacs. He could've been gone forever. Forever.

Derek took a step towards me. "Jordyn, what's all this? You gotta fiancé?" he asked with a puzzled look on his face.

"It's complicated." I said to him.

"No it's not. Do you or don't you have a fiancé?"

"Yes, but no. I mean, we were together, until I caught him cheating."

"Cheating?" Cavalli said quickly. "Cheatin'? And who was I cheatin' wit?" he asked with a half-believable look on his face.

I shook my head. I just knew he was gonna lie. Just knew it. But I was praying he didn't. I was praying for honesty, praying for him to be a man and tell me the truth. I felt like he at least owed me that.

"I saw you Cavalli. At Alexanders Strip Mall. The pizza parlor? You rubbing her hand, her smiling the same smile I used to smile when you touched me that way? But go head and lie. Lie to me, make it sound good. You're so good at that."

Cavalli didn't say a word, just smiled and started shaking his head. I wanted to say, *What the fuck so funny?*, but I held my stance, hand on my hip, jaw clenched, ready to fight. And on the other side was Derek and the goons. All staring at me, all awaiting my crazy response. But it wasn't what they were expecting, I'm sure. I never really had a potty mouth, and the words seemed to never come out right when I did want to cuss someone out. They were always twisted and unorganized.

"You stupid fuck! No shit's funny at all. You're a dumb mother-fucker. Stupid!"

Cavalli didn't speak, more head shakin' and smiling.

"I hate your lying, cheating, black ass, you clown! You're a no good piece of shit and you know it. Jackass fool!"

He kept smiling, shaking his head.

"What?!" I yelled. "Fuck is so funny?"

Cavalli got off one more shake and stepped closer. I balled my fist.

"Alexanders? Three weeks ago?" he asked smiling.

"Yeah. Alexanders. Three weeks ago? Pizza parlor. Dark-skinned chick? Big Chop hairstyle? Dimples? Piercing over her right eyebrow?"

"Lotta details, huh?"

"You got damn right you cheating bastard. So who was she and how long you been fuckin' her? Probably the whole time we been together, huh? Cheating bastard!"

Cavalli smiled again. But I wasn't smiling. I scowled.

"That's Keisha, Jordyn," he said plainly, as if I knew her.

"Keisha?!" I snapped. "And who the fuck is Keisha? You say her name like I know her."

"You do," he said plainly. "Keisha, as in my sister-in-law, Jordyn? My brother's wife?"

"OMG. So you're screwin' your brother's wife?" I said shaking my head. "Wow."

He laughed. "Girl, I ain't screwin' her."

"Sure. Then what were you two doin'? And why were you meeting her out there?"

"The prison my brother in ain't that far from there, Jordyn. You don't remember me telling you that a visit was comin' up, and he wanted to finally see you?"

"Yeah, and so what?"

"And she just came from seein' him, Jordyn." Cavalli took two steps closer. I shifted my weight to my left side. Good story, but he wasn't off the hook that easily. He could still get smacked. "They denied his appeal that day, Jordyn. She needed a little love."

"So you're not cheatin'?" I asked foolishly.

"No, I'm not cheatin', Jordyn. I love you girl."

"So what's with all the touchy-feely stuff then?"

"He got *lif,e* Jordyn. She needed some love, some consoling. That's my little sister, I love her. If it wasn't for her he'd be nothin' but a shell of a man. She givin' him a reason to wake up, Jordyn."

"So you're not cheating?" I asked again just to be sure.

"No, Jordyn, no. On my mother's soul I'm not cheatin'. I'm dealin' with way too much shit to be worryin' about another woman. Hell naw I ain't cheatin'."

I felt like a fool. That was Keisha, the woman who I'd held many telephone conversations with over the course of our relationship, but had never physically met. And whose fault was that? Mine. Every time Cavalli asked me to accompany him to the visit or out to lunch with her I'd always decline. But I always felt out of place. Now look. Look at me. The fool. I felt so stupid, so silly. I was embarrassed as hell. I couldn't believe it. I'd jumped to conclusions and made a fool out of myself. Fool! My ignorance and immaturity had bit me in the ass, and now I was standing there looking stupid. I wished I could've folded myself into a ball and rolled down into the drain. I was mortified, destroyed. I could feel the eyes of Derek and

Cavalli's goons searing into my flesh, but I couldn't bring myself to look at them. Especially Derek.

"Man this shit is whack!" said Derek and chirped the alarm to his car. "Your ass is as crazy as these two fools right here. Matter-of-fact, probably more. They get paid, you don't!" He spinned around, jumped in his car and screeched out of the parking lot.

Best thing he could've done, I thought.

"Jordyn, can we talk? In private?" Cavalli asked softly. "I really miss you, and I can't go on without you. These three weeks drove me crazy. I don't wanna lose you. Jus' get in and talk to me. Please."

The pity was obvious in Cavalli's eyes. I could see thousands and thousands of tiny speckles of pity dancing around like faux snowflakes in one of those tiny Christmas balls. He was serious, and I was dead wrong. DEAD WRONG. I owed him so much. And to think, I was about to have revenge sex against him. What a mistake that would've been. Geeze!

Cavalli and I sat in his car talking for an hour before Remy came back out to check on me. He'd come out about ten minutes afterwards, but I ensured him I was okay. Fifty minutes later, he was back checking on me.

"It's okay," I told Remy from the passenger side of Cavalli's white Range Rover Sport. "We're good, thanks."

Cavalli looked over me at Remy and stuck out his hand. "I apologize, Remy. I let my emotions get the best of me, and I'm extremely apologetic. It's just your cousin means the world to me, and… and, well, I'll just say this: Matters of the heart are unexplainable. But," he continued with his palm extended, "I'm a man and I can admit when I'm wrong." Remy looked down at Cavalli's hand then back over at me. My eyes were forgiving. So forgiving. I had caused a lot of BS in all of our lives and I just wanted it to be over.

Remy took Cavalli's hand. "No doubt," he said. "But don't let it happen again Cavalli. Jordyn means the world to me too, and I'll do whatever I have to to protect her. *Whatever,*" Remy said and shook Cavalli's hand firmly.

"No problem." Cavalli responded. "I understand. I do. And, no disrespect, but Jordyn comin' back home. I need her there Remy. Things just ain't the same without her."

Remy flashed a soft smile. "Who you tellin'? Well, If it's cool with Jordyn, it's cool wit' me. You good Jay-Jay?"

"Yeah, I'm good cuzin'. Just a little misunderstanding, on my behalf. I was wrong, I'll admit. And we're going on a vaca' real soon to get so things'll definitely be back in order. We're cool."

"You sure?" Remy asked.

"Positive. 100%."

"Alright. Call me later and check up on me," he said.

"Kay. Love you cuzin'."

Remy kissed me lightly on the forehead and Cavalli put the truck in gear.

I had my man back and I was sooo happy.

God is good!

<u>Chapter 14</u>

As soon as we got home, Cavalli booked a flight to Cabo San Lucas, no questions asked. There was no sex, no bickering back and forth between us. He booked a flight, stated his self more clearly—that, by no means was he cheating, whatsoever—and we mended our relationship. I was so ecstatic! All I wanted to do was be happy. Not make love or cook or clean; not pour through my closet and jewelry box to ensure I still had my "inheritance". No. I just want to smile and have a peaceful conversation with my man. And that we did. For six long hours we bonded, discussing everything and nothing alike, repairing the bridge that I'd damaged with my silly assumptions. And I'll tell you this: if I ever thought Cavalli was the man for me, this was the time. He held my hand and listened intently, then spoke back smoothly and eloquently, while I listened. Cavalli was my man got damnit, and I was back proud of being his woman!

*   *   *

So, we were off to Cabo San Lucas the following morning, and having caught little sleep, the puffy marshmallow clouds beneath us were a perfect backdrop for my slumber. No bags, no luggage, nothin' but the clothes on our backs. Don't be jealous. That's how it is when your engaged to a Hood Boss!

Cabo San Lucas was utterly beautiful. I mean beautiful! Clear blue waters, white sand, exotic wildlife, and sun bathed locales. I'm telling you, it was a sight like no other. I mean, the wildlife alone was anything more beautiful than I'd seen back home. As soon as we stepped foot from the plane I knew I could've spent my entire life there. There were Zip-lines everywhere, snorkeling exhibits, and I could tell at first sight that love making on that white sand would never get old to me.

I was dead hooked on Cabo!

Now, don't ask me how, but Cavalli already had a magnificent condo awaiting us when we arrived. It was located just off the beach and it was definitely something to cherish. I think it may've been a timeshare or something but I couldn't bring myself to ask him. I was just happy to be there with him. We were gonna be okay after this trip, I could feel it…

The second afternoon in Cabo a package arrived. It was a small brown box with thick clear tape and bore Cavalli's name. "Cavalli, baby, you got a package," I yelled from the front room of the condo. Cavalli was in the shower washing off our sex. I walked upstairs and rapped on the bathroom door and said it again. "You got a package, baby."

"A package?" he said kind of cluelessly, the running water muffling his voice a bit.

"Yeah. A small brown box," I said shifting the box around in my hands wonder what it could be.

"Who's it from?"

"No return address," I said and spinned the box around completely to see if maybe I'd overlooked it. "Nope, no address."

"Umm… A'ight, jus' put it on the mantle and I'll get it when I get out," he said. "Probably something from one on the locals or some shit. You come through and throw a couple of ones around and they treat you like you God."

Yeah, probably so, I thought, and placed the box on the mantle and I waited for Cavalli to finish showering before I took one of my own. I then dressed—in a designer dress that Cavalli picked out for me at this cute little boutique not far from there—and marveled at how gorgeous I looked. He'd spent $3800 on my dress and shoes alone, and boy did I feel penny of it. I looked good, smelled good, and so did my man. His taper was fresh as ever, waves bumpin' like those out on the beach, and his navy-blue suit was crisp and stunning. Cavalli's cufflinks shone like new money, alligator wingtips both flashy and classy, and his presidential Rolex had enough diamonds in it to blind the sun. We were the cutest couple alive, point blank period!

The sun was light and forgiving this day. The breeze blowing about was just enough to rustle a leave or two off of many indigenous Black Bark Santo trees that line the streets leading to the San De Ville Restaurant. We walked casually down the narrow street (that didn't seem much like a street at all) on our way to our private gazebo. /there were no parked cars or driveways to even park the cars in. It looked kinda weird to be frank. All the restaurant, shops, boutiques and stores were set back a-ways from the street—as if they were floating towards the sandy beaches— which made for the cutest picturesque backdrop. It was unbelievable. You could exit the backdoor of any restaurant or boutique on the strip and be in complete heaven. The serenity attached to the mist of the waves and the purity of the sand was enough to cause a person to go into shock. All I could say was: *beauty*. But the term "beauty" alone wasn't befitting of what I seen and felt there. It was something you couldn't put into words. The entire 200 yard trek from the condo to the restaurant felt like a dream; like I was floating upward to heaven, holding the hand of an angel, my head rested on the shoulder of a God. I'm telling you: this was an experience I'd never forget. As long as I lived I'd remember and appreciate this moment. This was an earthly interpretation of Heaven. I was back in love…

The gazebo was located in the rear of the club on the beach. It was covered with a thin sheer spread to ward off any pesky that wanted to feast on the tables-full of fresh seafood and fruit. Cavalli had covered every aspect. There were trays upon trays of appetizers and dessert, and the steamed beef and lamb and bottles of vintage wine arrived no soon as we sat.

"This is beautiful, baby," I said, looking around at everything then directly into his eyes.

"You like it?" he responded and took the seat across from me. "Anything for my baby. Anything!" he said.

I smiled and reached out for a piece of the dragon fruit. "Um. Fresh." Then a lobster tail.

Cavalli laughed. "You ain't wastin' no time here are you?"

"I'm starving," I said with a mouthful of butter-dipped lobster tail.

"Here," Cavalli said and laid a cloth napkin on the neckline of my dress.

"Thanks." But I didn't slow down. There was way too much delicious food in front of me to stop. And I was STARVING!

I put something on my stomach but never would I just sit up and gorge. I'm a lady first and was raised as one. Sure, sometimes Remy's side of me would come out and I'd stuff my jaws like a little gerbil. But, Tish's side would invade and I'd gather myself. And that's exactly what I did. I ate a few more pieces of lobster, and picked over a few other things, while Cavalli and I discussed our future over glasses of one-hundred year old wine. We spoke of places to retreat and retire after his last package was done, even a few lucrative business ventures that would make up for some of the fast money he was sure to be missing. And I knew it was gonna be a tough transition for him coming from all that profit annually, but, that's how life goes. Everything we want ain't always good for us, and too much of anything ain't either. Cavalli was a firm believer of this. And so, he gave his supplier his unofficial two weeks' notice a couple of days before we left. "I thought you left me because of the street shit," he admitted that night outside of Aphrodiacs. "So, shit, I said I was done. Even before I finished my shift, I said I was done. I told myself," he said looking at me in the eyes, "If this shit comin' between me and the only woman I ever gave a fuck about, it can't be good. And that was that. And yeah, I knew my connect was gone be pissed off that I was gone, but fuck 'em. You're the only person I owe my time and devotion to. They say if you can't stand for something you'll fall for anything. I can't lose you Jordyn. I can't. That's why I did it, why I brought you here, why I arranged all *this...*"

Cavalli waved his hand out towards the beach and a small group of convened. There were four flower girls, a tall man wearing a long robe, and a group of singing mariachis in short shorts and flower hats. There were two guys in black and white tuxedos carrying a red velvet throw, two chairs, and a small circular table. They moved swiftly towards us like trained professionals, and in an instant the most romantic setting I'd ever seen had been set up.

We arrived to the table just as the last few handfuls of white and red roses were scattered on the ground around our table. Right after, the dark-skinned gentleman bearing rosary beads and white and gold letter inscribed Holy Bible approached us. He had significant poise and weathered look about him but he looked to be spiritually at peace. He smiled and flipped his Bible open as we stopped before him.

"Greet-ings," he said in his deeply accented Caribbean voice. "May peace and understanding be wit' you, and may you be highly favored and chosen by the Most High God." Cavalli shook his hand and reached into his pocket.

How could I be so slow? I said to myself as Cavalli pulled the ring from his pocket. The robe, the Bible, the flowers, it all said marriage. And there wasn't a more sweet and romantic way for him to do it. All the exotic foods, the hundred year old wine and the roses made for a perfect day for me. There was no way I'd deny him. I was marrying this man, honey. And today!

Pastor Tibedu passed his hands over us gracefully. "Today I stand be-fore dese two bea-utiful peeples, ready 'n' willing to unite da two in hol-ey matrimony, under the power and ad-visement of tha peeple of the tenure of San Lucas, Cabo, and, respectfully, before the great eyes of da Lord… And this day, June Nine-teenth, Two-Tousand 'n' Tur-teen, I now pronounce you man and wife…"

Cavalli was so sensual when he pulled me closer and kissed me gently on the lips. He slid the flawless, pear-shaped 8 carat VVS Leo diamond on my ring finger and I caved. I was finally Mrs. Rico Cavalli, and there was nothing on earth that could take that from me. Nothing.\

* * *

After six or seven more bluesy songs and two more glasses of vintage wine, Cavalli and I rode a horse carriage to a private villa that sat in the center of the beach. We had awesome sex and watched the stars until we fell asleep. I was proud to be his wife. Very, very proud.

<u>Chapter 15</u>

After a traditional Cabo breakfast (one of poached eggs, fresh dragonfruit and papaya and fresh Figi fish), Cavalli and I had slow sensual sex and headed back to the condo. And lemme tell you: I was happy! Finally I had fulfilled the dream. I had my dream man, my dream ring, and even though the wedding wasn't the exact I'd envisioned and dreamed of, it was amazing and I loved it. I never expected any of this. Never in my dreams would my life to be this perfect. Never. I was living a story book fairy tale, and, if it was up to me, the last chapter would never be finalized. There'd be a limitless supply of love and sex, and before long, children. A boy and a girl and I wanted them close in age. I wanted them to live, love, and bond with one another like siblings are supposed to. But, like everything else in life, all things don't go as we plan...

*   *   *

"I could live here forever!" I said happily as we walked into the condo. Cavalli let me pass around him while he removed the key from the knob. I laid my bag down on the chaise. "I'm telling you babe. The people, the food, the water. Um," I said and spinned around. "I'd be truly happy here. Just me, you, and..."
Suddenly I noticed the box I'd left on the mantel sitting in the middle of the floor just past the foyer. I stopped in my

tracks, my eyebrows knitted together. Cavalli was still near the door, I could hear his footsteps.

"Um, bay, did you grab the box from mantel?" I asked, knowing full well he hadn't. It still looked to be unopened, just no other explanation (outside of someone breaking in) to explain *how* it got there.

Cavalli walked up behind me and rest his hands on my shoulders, his pelvis pressed against my butt. "Huh?" he asked in my ear.

"The box," I said pointing down at it. "Did you put it there?"

Cavalli paused. Not a good pause either; one that, for just a moment, underlined the fact that something bad was happening.

"Nah," Cavalli said with a cautious step from around me. "Huh-un. But um…"—I could hear the frog in his throat— "Let's see what it is…"

Cavalli walked casually over to the box and bent down. He picked up the box and analyzed it. "No return sender," he mused.

"I know. That's what I was telling you." And for some reason I had a bad feeling. I watched Cavalli take and tear open the tape, moving aside a piece of white tissue paper. His eyebrow scrunched up much like mine.

"What?" I asked, the worry in my voice obvious. "What is it?"

Cavalli reached in and removed the tissue paper completely to get a better look. "Fuck," he said and shook his head.

I took two steps and leaned in to get a better look "What babe? What is it?"

Cavalli removed a small brown object with a white piece of paper strung to it and let the box fall to the floor. It bounced twice and landed near my right foot. "They got her," was all he said. "They fuckin' got her."

I stepped a little closer. "Who? They got who, Babe?" I was clueless as to what was going on, but I could feel the negativity in the air. Something was definitely wrong.

Cavalli dropped his head. "What?" I asked now just feet from him. At first sight I gasped and covered my mouth. "Oh my God. Is that?…"

"Its Keisha's, baby. They killed her and sent me her fucking ring finger."

I looked at the pretty chocolate finger and the flawless three carat diamond ring attached to it and my stomach turned over. A tiny tear of blood stained the note and another smeared the pear-shaped diamond attached to the white gold post. This was real.

"But?… Who? … Why? …" Was all I could muster. A tear dropped from Cavalli's eye as he reached down and picked the box back up. He very gently laid the finger back inside and pulled out his cell. He dialed ten digits and put the phone on speaker mode.

"Ah, so, Mr. Cavalli," was what emanated from the phone. "So I see you got my message, hey?" His accent was thick, of Hispanic origin, and he spoke with an air of arrogance and nefariousness that only a true crime boss could mimic. I could tell off bat that he was somebody; that the underworld was his element. I looked back towards the door then back at Cavalli.

"Why, El Hefe? Why? Why you do it for man? She ain't deserve this shit man and you know it?"

"Oh do I? And what make you think somethin' like that Cavalli? Because she pretty?" he said sarcastically. "Or, or, because she marry you brother? I told you there'd be consequences for disloyalty."

"Disloyalty? Fuck was I ever disloyal to you? Huh? When? I made you more money than any of 'em dem half-ass hustlaz you got in the Midwest and you know it. Five million a month, Hefe. Five mill and never have I crossed you, clipped you, or said any fuck shit behind your back. I did nuttin' but be loyal to you, and this the fuckin' thanks I get?"

He chuckled "You get out of this life what you put in."

"And what did I put in to deserve this? What, because I wanted out? Because I want a life outside of this shit? One where I ain't gotta worry about fuckin' packages like THIS!

"It's wrong for you to think it was so easy Cavalli. You were like a son to me. I loved you like Hernandez, my wife's kid. But you didn't reciprocate. Now you pay."

"What do you want from me?!" Cavalli yelled. "What? Money? You want my retirement package? Is that what you want?"

The man known as El Hefe laughed. "Money? Ha! You giving me money? Be serious. I have enough money for ten lifetimes. Don't make more of a fool of yourself."

"Well what do you want?"

"For you to maintain your obligation, Cavalli," he said plainly. "For you to be a man of your word."

"Obligation? My word? I aint got no more obligations with you. I paid you everything I owed you and I ain't accept the last package. So what obligation I got besides being my own man and being there for my family."

"Ha! There it goes. Family. Exactly! Family. That's what this is all about. That's why we're havin' this conversation Mr. Cavalli. My family is troubled by your sudden need for departure. And why? You've obliged us for ten long years, and our families back home have grown to love and trust you. They've grown comfortable with the services you provided, and they wonder what life outside of the streets would be like for you. They wonder about the residual effects of your departure Mr. Cavalli. Have you ever thought about that? What if everybody decided they wanted to run off? Huh? What then? Where would we be then? And what about all the work it took for you to maintain what you grew to love? Do you think there is no consequences back home for us? Have you not seen CNN and the World News, watched the heads of politicians and button pushers stacked up the city streets? That's what I mean by obligation. This life is bigger than you Mr. Cavalli. Much bigger. And if you want your life—And the life of your pretty new wife—you'd comply. Otherwise, be prepared to dress your families in black."

Cavalli looked back at me. I could see the fury and wrath in his eyes. He wanted to kill this man, whoever he was, and it was written all over his face. He clenched down his jaws, his nostrils flared out like two hate-filled and he closed his eyes. "Come and get me Hefe, come and fuckin' get me…"

<u>Chapter 16</u>

The flight back from Cabo San Lucas was so sullen and spirit draining that all I could do was close my eyes and pretend to sleep. Every ripple in the sky, every bump in turbulence, and my mind was somewhere else. It wasn't fair! I didn't deserve this—Keisha didn't deserve it—and all I could think of was how her blood was stained on that wedding ring. Suddenly the weight from my own wedding ring was enormous to me. It reminded me of the unfairness and brutality of the streets, the fact that no matter how hard you fight, how unbiased you are to the negativities that encircle the life, the streets will always win. And I don't even know if Keisha was involved in her husband's nefarious lifestyle. What I do know is however the residual effect returned to haunt her. I also know that everything that ever separated the two was brought back full surface by the anatomy of the streets... Every element ever indulged in came back to bite her in the end. Yes, she paid for every diamond, every foreign vehicle, and every expensive handbag he'd ever purchased for her... Every acre she lived on, every vacation, and every spa day. And she paid with her life! It was a damn shame, and to be honest, once again, I was second guessing my decision of being with Cavalli. *Would I be next? Would he ever make it out?,* I thought. I wanted to turn and look over at Cavalli (who opted for the isle seat, giving me the window), and fix his broken spirit with my soft, understanding eyes. But I couldn't. I just couldn't. I didn't want those eyes staring back at me. Not now, not then. Those eyes bore pain, anguish, and a general fear of what was to come. I couldn't imagine what was going through his mind at that time. But I knew we couldn't run forever…

*   *   *

The tension was so thick back home that you could literally cut it with a knife. Cavalli shuffled through the house with a scowl on his face, lips curled tightly, on his waist the biggest handgun I'd ever seen in my life. It was black and grey with a long piece of plastic protruding from its handle, and Cavalli gripped it tightly. He paced back and forth, back and forth through our mini-mansion, checking windows and doors cautiously as I packed our bags. Our home had become a place of fear and worry, and every second that passed the suspense grew thicker. I'd occasionally check over my shoulder for danger, knowing very well that a team of heavily armed Mexican gangsters could pour through the front door and pelt us with bullets. I could envision the anger etched on their brown faces, the tight grips on their guns and the bright flashes from their muzzles… I could hear the pops and bangs reverberating through the house as they shot us, the painful sizzle the hot bullets made as they tore into our flesh and broke apart our bones. I could *hear the damage*, *feel* the damage, *see* it. Something very bad was about to happen, I could feel it. I quickly packed, jumped in the passenger side of the Mercedes, and buckled in.

Cavalli smashed the gas.

Death was in the air …

*   *   *

When we pulled up outside of Jordyn's the number of cars out back let me know that Born Seven's Party was a success. Why, out of all places would a best-selling author of nine books choose our establishment to promote his new product, I don't know. But, I can say that I did my job as an event planner. *Too bad I wasn't going to be around to enjoy it,* I thought, and grabbed the door handle to my establishment.

"We clearin' the safes and we out," Cavalli instructed. "We aint got time for anything else."

"But to where, Cavalli? Why are we running if you didn't do anything?" I asked in a whiny pout.

Cavalli's face tightened. "I ain't neva ran from a ma'fucka in my life, and I neva will! I jus' know how dese ma'fuckaz rock, and I don't wanna lose you."

"But where will we go?" I asked.

"I got some property outside of Columbus. You can stay there while I get shit settled here. I'ma smooth this shit out, and—"

Suddenly three black SUVs whipped into the parking lot, their tires coming to a screeching halt fifty yards away from us. White smoke filled the air and their doors flew open.

"Baby," I said in a whimper.

"Go! Hurry! Inside!" Cavalli yelled and cocked back the slide on his pistol, stepping out to protect me as I ran inside. I could see the Mexicans—heavily armed—jumping out of their vehicles as I ran towards the entrance of Jordyn's. And if there was ever an awkward moment, it was then, when I passed through the double doors of my own club. Everyone inside either knew of me personally (from the club) or knew of me as the owner of the establishment. So, to see me burst through the front door, panicked and worry-stricken, rushing to the back office, my eyes popped out of my head like I'd just been stabbed in the back, it had to be startling. It was crazy. I'd unintentionally commanded the attention of everyone inside, and if I myself didn't grab their attention—and hold it like a burglar with a bag of stolen jewels—then Cavalli bursting through the door, handgun clutched, checking over his right shoulder as if he were ready to begin firing—did. Our eyes connected and again he yelled. "Go! Go!" he said as I ran into the back office towards the safes. I quickly filled my bag with bundles of cash and checks, then bent down to empty the floor safe. Just as I removed the rug, exposing the shiny titanium face of the electronic fire-proof safe, I heard a pop. Then another, and another. Within seconds there was a cacophony of non-sequential gun blasts filling the inside of Jordyn's. It was bad. Very bad. And although I was hoping for the best, the truth was Cavalli was out-numbered and his enemies' guns were much bigger and dangerous. They were probably hired assassins with specific orders to kill my husband for wanting to retire from the lifestyle. And what about me? I'd heard with my own ears El Hefe say kill the both of us. So what was I to do? What? Two of Cavalli's pistols were inside the floor-safe—along with a handful of rare gems and coins—but what was the likelihood that I'd be able to ward them off all by myself? I could feel it in my chest, I was about to die. I knew it.

God please protect me from my enemies, I prayed. *You are my Rock, my everything. Protect me Father…*

*   *   *

Sirens loomed in the distance, mixing with the sobs and cries on the other side of my office door. I checked the chamber on the pistol to ensure it was loaded and secured the bag to the top of my arm. With a bag full of cash, blank checks and priceless gems and coins, I exited the office door. And what I saw ruined me. Five or six people lay on the ground bleeding, patrons over top aiding and assisting with their wounds. Near the entrance lay two of three Mexicans, bleeding, groaning, their lives nearly emptied from their bodies. But where was Cavalli? Where was my husband? Where was—

Wait! There he was, standing against one of the African warrior statues, holding his shoulder. From the manner in which he stood, the statue seemed to serve as a shield, a true protector of hearts and souls of black men, women, and children. I looked at Cavalli and the tears started pouring. He was hit. He was hurt. *But how bad?* I wondered, as I scurried over to his rescue. His designer clothing had been ruined with blood and seared skin, and the stained diamonds on his neck and wrist gave literal meaning to the words "blood diamonds". I bent down and scooped him up, wrapping his injured arm over my shoulder to support him. Cavalli winced and groaned, then rose his weapon. He aimed and pulled the trigger. *Boom! Boom! Boom, Boom, Boom!*

"Ahhhhh!"I yelled overtop of the remaining seven or ten patrons left inside the club. Some were wounded and almost helpless, while the others attended to them. Everyone braced as the bullets rang out and puffs of smoke leapt from the chest of a Mexican. He spit out a mouthful of blood, dropped his weapon to the floor and fell back to the ground smacking his head against imported tiling. He was dead, definitely dead.

"I got you Baby," Cavalli muttered. "I told you… I'd never let anything, anything ever happen to you. You're my world, my life… You're my… My… My…" Cavalli groaned and his body went limp.

I knew death was in the air…

Chapter 17

I made it out of the parking lot just seconds before the band of police vehicles screeched in. Their tires jumped the small hump leading into the lot and it seemed like before their vehicles had even stopped, that they were out with their guns drawn. I watched them through the rearview for as long as I could, then, just as I lost sight if them, in came to view the E.M.T.'s.

Thank God, I said to myself. *I pray everyone's alright. I pray everyone is—* moans from the passenger side broke my thought pattern.

"Are you okay, Baby? Oh my God! I need to get you to a hospital. Hold on baby, we almost there."

"No hospi—no hospitals," he managed to say.

"But you're bleeding, everywhere."

"No hospitals," he said and shut his eyes and slumped over against the door. His entire shirt was soiled with crimson blood, and he was weak. I had to. Even though he was against it, I had to. I had to get help. He was probably gonna hate me for my decision, but preserving his life was all that mattered to me. Forget street etiquette and logic, and forget the cops. All I knew was I needed him alive, that he couldn't die on me. What would I do, who would I be without him? Ever since he came into my life I'd been happy—truly, truly happy. And I couldn't see my life the same without him. I had to take him to the hospital. Now!

*   *   *

Cavalli suffered a collapsed lung and a ruptured spleen. He had tubes running in and out of him on three different parts of his body, and a machine regulated his breathing. My Baby was clinging on to his life, and the worst part about it had yet to come. The petty-ass cops came in and served him an indictment. Murder, felonious assaults, firing a firearm in a liquor establishment, even charged *me* for tampering with evidence! They claimed that I removed a murderer, a felon—along with evidence that would assist with their investigation—from the crime scene. I was served my indictment and told to appear in court right alongside Cavalli. Problem was, they slapped cuffs on him right then and there. Petty! Clipped his murder indictment to his E.R. chart. Petty. Just petty! Then advised the night watchman to ensure he didn't leave.

"He disappears and it your arse," said the white bushy eye-browed older man with black eyes, brown dockers and a short-sleeved button-up shirt and Canadian accent. He pointed his finger directly in the night watchman's face—a young white guy of no more than eighteen years old, with no facial hair, red spiky hair and braces on his teeth—and reminded, "Your arse!" before exiting the room.

I could see the anger dancing around inside of Cavalli's eyes. He was infuriated with me for bringing him there, must've known the outcome, foreseen the shiny bracelets on his wrist, and the indictment clipped to the E.R. chart. But I wonder if he knew he wouldn't have made it without me. I wonder if he knew he wouldn't have survived a good two hours on the streets without the proper medical attention. I wonder if, through his anger, he could see that? Probably not. But he didn't need those types of thoughts running through his head. He needed consoling. Keisha was dead already, he was laying up in a hospital bed, fighting for his life, and we were both facing serious felony charges. True enough Cavalli's were more serious than mine, but I was damaged now too. I laid my hand on my husband's and rubbed his knuckle. Cavalli was my, Baby and I loved him.

<u>Chapter 18</u>

At midnight the watchman switched post with another guy, I think the one from food court. He was about the same age, build (slim), and seemed to be just as unenthusiastic about working as the other guy. They exchanged keys and walkie-talkies, said their goodbyes, and the new guy went to the restroom, to, I suppose, prepare himself for his 8 hour shift. I took a sip of water, and reclaimed my spot next to my man. I had a lot of things running through my mind. Cavalli, our future, his health, and all types of other stuff. My temples pulsated with the worst headache I'd ever had, and my stomach had a weird uneasy feeling, almost as if I'd drank bad milk or eaten sesame seeds. I was allergic to sesame, and every time I so much as come close to a sesame seed my stomach would become uneasy and I'd throw up. Suddenly I felt that way. My stomach churned and vomit began to force its way up my esophagus.

I covered my mouth and ran to the restroom.

While I was bent over the toilet, a lot of things were running through my mind. *What's gonna happen from here? Will he survive? Did he deserve this?* I felt horrible in a way for going against his word, but then in the same token, I felt as though I saved his life. I was conflicted , and I didn't know what was right or wrong. All I knew was no matter what, I was there and so was he. So what if we were indicted to be charged and possibly gonna face jail time. I truthfully didn't care. As long as I had my husband, and as long as we were still one. I was cool. We were a team, and that's all that mattered to me. That's all that fucking mattered…

I exited the bathroom after freshening to find Cavalli napping. He looked uncomfortable and in constant pain. But I found pleasure in just seeing him there. He could've been one of those dead bodies outlined in chalk back there at Jordyn's. He could have been shot dead, gone, forever, and then what? Then what? So, yes, I was happy he was there with me. He was there with me, in the flesh, and I was ecstatic. So what we were to be charged? So what life would never be the same in the sense of normalcy. I was there with him and that's all that mattered. That's all that mattered!!!

When I sat down next to Cavalli, I noticed a man standing in my peripheral. He wore a dark service uniform similar to the watchman, but not identical. His boots were dirty—a little too dirty to suit his profession—and his jacket was a little too thick for the weather. Something about his eyes wasn't right either. Suddenly, I wondered where the other watchmen went. I stood to see if I could see him outside the door. That's when the guy with the dirty boots faced me. His eyes gave him away immediately. They were dark— too dark—and squinty with black rings underneath. He opened his jacket and reached. The silencer attached to the end of his weapon was the first thing I noticed. The second was the flame from its tip. I threw myself over Cavalli to shield him from the bullets. With each one that entered my back and side I gripped him tighter, and with every shot I became closer to him.

I looked him in his eyes as I faded.

His sweet brown iris was the last sight before my eyes.

I can now say that I've lived and died, in love…

<u>Epilogue</u>

I awoke some three odd weeks later with tubes of my own down my throat and nose, and I.V.'s in my arm. A metallic taste saturated my tongue and mouth, and my throat stung when I tried to swallow. I'd been shot four times with a 9mm Beretta, and suffered similar injuries as my husband. I had a damaged lung, femur, and they killed my child. I didn't even know I was pregnant. Come to find out, I was two months, expecting my first child, with my first and only love, Cavalli.

Speaking of him, he pulled through rather quickly. From what doctors said, we were both guarded by angels. We were both hit in vital organs, both on life support for nearly a week, and both survived. I cried for days about my lost child—and my life as a whole—but in the end, there was nothing I could do. It was all spilled milk. My unborn child was dead and gone, Cavalli was facing a laundry list of felony charges (including two counts of murder), and I was being charged with a felony of the 3rd degree. But like I said, I never anticipated marrying a gangster. I never asked—or even wanted—to be involved in his mannish lifestyle. All I wanted was love, respect, and affection; for him to be my best friend and companion; my knight in shining armor; my everything and more. But I guess we don't always get what we want and desire from life. We do live and we learn though. We live, we learn, and we grow. Because everybody dies, but not everybody lives…

By: Ms. Juicy C & Hector Tha Plug

Also available on EDUCATED THUG PUBLICATIONS

Street Royalty 937 "Im So Sincere"
Street Royalty 937 "Seven Takes Over"
Omerta
The Incarcerated 7's Anthology

Coming soon
Pound 4 Pound "An Educated Thug Tale
Redemption"
Omerta 2
Black Rose
Memoir of a Poetic Prisoner 1 & 2
Rico

www.ingramcontent.com/pod-product-compliance
Lightning Source LLC
Chambersburg PA
CBHW051251170626

46809CB00004B/1601